I
al

C000193068

Dedication: this book is for all those free in
spirit, with open minds that can understand
and enjoy the adventures of living – both the
good and the bad.   *R J Small*

Published by
Goodnessmepublishing.co.uk

About the author.

If you read the Porlock Weir story you will
find out what sort of person he is; his ideals,
motives and beliefs.

Other books by the same author

I want to tell you a story
Edward Gaskell Publishers
Ghosts and Things
Edward Gaskell Publishers
Tales from Merlin's Pal
Edward Gaskell Publishers
Simple Poems
Edward Gaskell Publishers
Reflections on a tai chi journey
Goodnessmepublishing.co.uk
Aikido weapons and principles
Goodnessmepublishing.co.uk

Contents.

Appledore

A Winter's Night on Irsha Street.

Comfortingly back home in my contemporary kitchen, doors locked tight and electric lights all on, ... I sit with my elbows resting on my old pine table, its enduring strength a reassuring prop to my insecurities. My much loved table, despite its many sufferings, it has stood the test of time. I feel the warmth from the log fire sending out its comforting glow across the room, the burning wood crackling a song of the forest, accompanied by a hushed but harmonious howling as air is drawn through small iron vents . Both the table and fire somehow seem to connect me to the past, with happy memories of days that were for me perhaps not as durable. I pick up a note book and begin to write for you, though my senses are still somewhat puzzled by the events that occurred during a visit I made earlier that evening to a little place called Irsha Street.

Irsha, almost a place that time has forgotten, was a quaint little street in a remote old fishing village. Irsha is long and narrow, with only a car width road and no pavements; many small alley ways disappear left and right into a darkness that has dwelled for centuries between the houses, some paths disappear inland towards the hill and some out towards the sea. The houses on one side of Irsha stand elevated from the sea on a cliff like stone sea wall. Lower down, even closer to the sea, once stood other old seafarer's houses, but these had failed to endure tide and time and stand no more; no trace remains, as if they never were.

As I write this, something is telling me that I am not entirely alone in this seemingly empty kitchen, something gently touches the crown of my head as if to say they know what I am doing, ... perhaps a warning, but there is no sense of dread, not this time, just a presence that has joined me from where I know not and nor why.

In any event, alone or accompanied, I'll still share with you of my visit.

"Call in for a cup of tea sometime," Joe had said.

So, on this wet winter's night, as occasional drizzle drifted here and there dropping gentle rain on the nearby rugged Devon coast, I thought it time I accepted his kind offer.

I left my car in the poorly lit and deserted quayside car park, put on my long black overcoat and adjusted my scarf and woolly hat against the damp. As I walked alongside the waterfront railings into the darkness towards Irsha, pinpoints of coloured light brightened the murk far across the bay; warnings to sailors of sandbars and rocks; sparkling beacons distant in a dark foreboding sea. As I entered Irsha Street the wind dropped and all became hushed, even my shoes on the tarmac were strangely silent, as were the many houses I passed on either side. The street itself was deserted; and seemingly so were most of the houses, only one or two showed a light, and even then no one was to be seen through the glass, I didn't like to peer inside for fear of someone looking out only to be disturbed by such ill mannered intrusion.

Directions and landmarks I'd been given soon led me to the house I sought; it was pleasantly easy to find in fact.

It was dark in Irsha except for the few dim street lights that sporadically lit the narrow roadway; a roadway wet from earlier rain that evening. There was a light on in the house and I could clearly see through the window I had found the right place; my host was sitting in a large chair in the far left corner of what appeared surprisingly to be quite a large room. I soon found the door, and knocked.

I didn't have to wait long before the door opened and a smiling face greeted me.

"Come on in," Joe said, "come on through."

I bowed my head through the low doorway and entered.

Once inside, I found the house was much larger than I had anticipated, I previously thought that they were all small two up two down cottages along Irsha. As is so often the case, what we think we see isn't what we think it is. There's many a surprise in life for us all about what we thought we saw. The entrance lobby and first room through which we walked was unlit, except for light coming through an opening to the next room, but I could still see the beamed ceiling, tasteful furniture and paintings. Underfoot I felt the cold and uneven flags of the 16thC stone floor. We moved through the opening into a similarly presented room. My host, a worldly wise, stocky and affable man of some years was talking to someone that I could not see. It all became clear as he ushered me through a low opening to yet more rooms at the back and there was the lady of the house, the partner to his conversation, quietly making tea. She was a pleasantly positive and talkative lady who invited me to remove my coat and sit a while and 'did I want sugar in my tea'?

'That's a relief,' I thought, at least he's not talking to imaginary people; or worse still, something else of which my mind would rather stay in ignorance.

It was a large and interesting back room, with a central inglenook fireplace complete with old ironmongery for hanging meat and cooking pots. All around were misshapen ancient walls, on which paintings of seascapes and sailing ships hung as testimony to a maritime past, and floors that leaned this way and that in no particular order. As my tea slowly went cold in my hands my host's conversation continued absorbingly, with tales of smugglers, murders, secret tunnels and of footsteps heard crossing the wooden floors of the empty rooms above. Joe spoke quietly of these things in the manner of a man that knew the truth of this world.

Once an old inn, both the building and its contents smacked of another age. It was almost as though I had gone back in time, as though the energy left by the past was still present and willing to show itself. The conversation led me to sense that I too might 'see', 'hear' or 'feel' the past. After tea I was shown around the labyrinth of rooms and stairs of all shapes in which many a hiding place could remain a secret for all times. I stood on steps where once stood the murdered excise officer and I walked the floor over which many a contraband barrel had rolled, I looked to the walls and floors, beyond which lay secret places and hidden history, in part I felt that my soul saw more than my eyes.

How often have we glimpsed something from the corner of our eye but when we look again there is nothing there … or was there? The child that plays with imaginary friends, or sees something in the night, is soon put right by the knowing and fearful adult. ….. "best not to look … no, no, don't look, … don't tell me any more … there's nothing there …. Go to sleep, close your eyes."

Whose eyes is it that were really closed?

Another cup of tea and the invisible hours had passed us by, as though they never were ....

I picked up my nearly drunk tea ... the cup was cold to my touch ......"Gosh, is that the time?" I said, glancing at the digital watch on my wrist, "I really must be away home and leave you in peace; thank you so much for your timeless hospitality, most interesting," ... and, reflecting upon their revelations, thinking privately, 'and almost beyond belief too'.

I bid farewell and re-crossed the 16th Century stones to the door with Joe, the gentleman of the house. He too seemed timeless, as though he were part of the fabric of the old Inn himself, at one with the hostelry, attuned to the heartbeat of the house that held so many secrets.

Buttoning my long dark overcoat it seemed to fit me better than when I'd arrived, I somehow felt taller, more comfortable and strong, as though younger now, almost like being someone else. I stepped into the rain damped narrow street, the old Inn door closing quietly behind me.

I began a silent, contemplative walk eastwards along the hushed and still deserted Irsha. My mind wandered to the events of the evening, then I glimpsed something from the corner of my eye; something large that loomed out of the darkness. My eyes slowly accustomed to the night and a faint breeze carried the smell of salt air to my nostrils and the creaking of timbers and rigging to my ears .... as the darkness was eased apart by shifting clouds a faint moonlight revealed an ancient ship of two masts riding newly at anchor in the deep water channel, rolling so gently in harmony with the tireless estuary waves, her sails furled, ... I thought I saw movement on deck, thought I saw the swing of the hurricane lamp, ... and then nature drew its curtain of clouds once more to hide the moon and I was left with a darkness within a darkness and the sound of water lapping the rocks. A previously unknown knowing came in to my head, she was a Brigantine, yes, that's what she was, a Brigantine, two masted and shallow draft .... and not long home from sea too.

If she was truly there or not, now I cannot say, but that night I knew exactly where she was, how tall, how rigged and all such detail that could be seen and told.

All was made more real by the clearly audible, slow soporific swoosh of gentle waves lapping the shore in slow rhythm, with the pauses between almost as though the sea were holding its breath.

As I passed by the little slipway I sensed three men, short and stocky, wearing mufflers and caps, heaving their fully laden row boat further up the stone slip, for the tide was still not yet passed to the ebb. I did not linger to watch, but somehow intuition told me what they were doing; contraband. How thankful I was now that I had left the house when I did, this was no place for the faint hearted and those men would not be best pleased to be discovered.

The spectre of a long gone past began to haunt Irsha, and I edged nearer the middle of the empty street for safety. I walked on quietly not wishing to disturb what was happening, yet slightly fearful and knowing I could no longer turn back, it was as if I had entered the sorcerer's cave and now fear to wake him.

Irsha is long and narrow but this night it seemed ever more so, time seemed confused in some way, the street, like time, never seeming to end. Then something walked alongside me, I became aware of two men, who though strongly built seemed of a desperately nervous disposition; their nailed boots trod not on tarmac but on rutted stones and there was a fleeting whiff of rotting vegetation and sewage in the air as if it lay in the street. They walked in a greater darkness than I. It would appear that the men did not see me, or if they did I meant nothing to them. Nothing I saw seemed to see me, a cloak of timely invisibility covered me, though at times I feared it would not.

I became aware of the untidy ramshackle quay side with its frames, boxes and nets and the river beyond as though there were now no houses between me and they.

I walked on and on, passing some small houses that seemed no more than pauper's hovels and into one of which both men vanished. It was as though they never were, except that the sound of their voices lingered on, it was the last thing to pass ... a curse it was, 'twas press gangs working the town that they cursed, ... then their voices followed them into their greater silence, and Irsha was quiet again.

Driven by an unexpected and transient gust of wind some smoke drifted across the street; the smell of wood smoke filled the air and my now heightened senses. I moved on, still slow and in a silence, sensing, as I passed by, places born of centuries past itself, the shivers, the hunger, the fear, a sense of little expectation from life but to survive, a sense of those waiting in vain but always in hope of a loved son's return from the sea.

I walked out of Irsha and towards the Church and its graveyard. There, no doubt, we might find our ghosts' ageing bones but so often the poor can leave no markers except in our hearts. We may still be touched by their troubled spirits even today, if we did but take notice.

Somehow transformed by my journey into Irsha, words of noble poetry and stories of the soul sprang eagerly to mind and those words triggered feelings. Not unlike hearing songs or stories that can fill us all with feelings. Feelings as if we were still there, like when we were young; feelings that connect us to our own past and even to our own ancestors and a knowing what they must have done and felt …. For in part, we are them. In our mind we can belong to a different place and time … even if for a brief while, for a glimpse is all we need in order to 'know' …..
You must have been there yourself; you must

have felt this in your own being sometime, somewhere. ....

Irsha was well behind me now and I carried only memories with me towards the live music that came from the local pub. To my left a glint of Moonlight, which had evaded the clouds, crossed the river to the street lights of Instow.

The pub was full of friendly people enjoying the warmth of drink and music, the bar was full of life. Warm applause greeted the rag tag and bobtail group of musicians as the song ended, leaving me with residual feelings ..... feelings that were trapped briefly in time past .... Once again I felt the strength of my youth and the courage of my forebears, my mind had transcended time and distance if only for a while. I ordered a Guinness from the bar and I reflected on an old saying, 'if the end is part of the story, then death is a part of living,' .... Perhaps we too will 'live on' somehow too. .....

"The end of anything is never a stopping point;
It is merely the doorway to new discoveries".

Appledore

The Resolute Coxswain.
(A lifeboat rescue story like no other.)

Old George Millar was a popular grocer in the little fishing village. His shop, with its worn boarded floor and evocative smells of package free food and spices, was like a place that time had left behind. Now in his eightieth year, kindly George Millar still served, driven on by a secret he'd kept for fifty years and compelled by conscience never to give up.

George straightened the frayed collar of his soft and comfortable shop coat, returned to the wooden counter and added freshly cut cheese to the contents of his customer's cotton shopping bag. 'There you go, young Andrew, you'll not be short of something for tea now and just the job for a snack after a call out. Has the boat been busy lately?'

Andrew, with his several years experience at sea, was second coxswain for the village's all-weather lifeboat. It was a job he loved dearly and, like many of his forebears, always felt he was born to it. 'No, nothing much happened this week, Mr Millar, just a shout to surfers who were taken along the shore by the rip tide. Just as well that it's quiet too, this being early March, the skipper is away for a week's training in Dorset, possibly a new boat coming our way later in the year is my guess. Mind you, the weather forecast is not good for later today. Rapidly strengthening winds with a cold front from the east they say, that'll keep the surfers on shore, even the wild ones.'

'And indoors in some nice warm hostelry no doubt,' smiled the affable old shopkeeper, 'and who could blame them?' Then his face darkened and the smile disappeared, 'Of course, I knew your grandfather Robert well. A dreadfully sad day it was when we lost him. He was a first-rate coxswain and a good man indeed. When the alarm beckoned him to sea for some poor soul in need, you never found him wanting, he wouldn't give up until he found them you know. Might be what cost him so dear in the end.' George was staring intently at an empty space in the shop as though looking in disbelief at a wild but empty ocean, to this day still looking frantically for some sign of a life that was already long extinguished. 'It was a day much like this one Andrew, I tell you, just like this one.' George Millar often repeated his sad tale, forgetting he'd told it so many times before. From that day on, he'd lived racked with a sense of guilt and a haunting memory from which this old man seemed never to be free.

Andrew always humoured him, never letting on. They all knew how George Millar had punished himself all these years, 'I don't remember him, Mr Millar, I'm sad to say he died before I was old enough. Dad has told me many a tale of his exploits though, so I feel that I do know him. We have a few photographs of course and I almost see him before me when dad tells his stories. I suppose his tales are born of truth, duty and tragedy and as such, they'll always carry something of the spirit with them, something undying. They're stories that will live forever.

Both stood humbly quiet for a minute or more, their shared silence suddenly broken by a rapid bleeping. Instinctively Andrew slipped the pager from his belt and read the message. . . it simply said, 'launch all-weather boat.'

'Must go Mr Millar, we've got a shout, keep my groceries for me, see you later,' and with that, the old shop door rattled closed and he was gone.

'Stay safe boy, stay safe,' muttered George. He knew only too well what might be waiting for his brave friends in the gathering storm. A gust of wind beat at his shop door. George Millar sighed. Picking up the bag to place it in the fridge, he muttered to himself, 'A day just like this, just like this.'

Andrew was not first to arrive at the lifeboat station, the mechanic was already there and dressed. Engine running, the tractor was parked on the slipway with the transfer boat waiting on its trailer.

'Local boat called it in Andrew, it's the *Anne-Clare*, crew of three, one man overboard, half mile off the west point of Anchor Rocks, they have fishing gear out and retrieving it now,' he shouted, pointing to a sheet of paper he held out towards Andrew.

Andrew lifted a hand in silent acknowledgement and entered the locker room to collect his dry suit and life jacket. 'Fishing gear out,' he thought, 'that'll slow them down, no wonder they've called for us.' Andrew knew Mark the skipper of the *Anne-Clare* quite well, they'd been to school together and some of Mark's family had also served on the village's earlier lifeboats, *Princess Dauntless* and the *Jocelyn.* It was a sad *Princess Dauntless* that had slunk home from the sea without his grandfather all those years before.

Andrew shook himself out of such thoughts and called for a crew of six from the rapidly gathering volunteers. Integrity and a common purpose overriding any personal desires or fears, it was not long before the chosen few were afloat and motoring out in the transfer boat to the deep water channel.

There, like a straining dog on a leash, the Tamar-class lifeboat rocked impatiently in the waves as though eager to be slipped from her mooring.

They faced a spring tide, running strong and rising fast at nearly half flood. Conditions that meant the ocean currents around Anchor Rocks would be even more dangerous than usual. They were going to have to hurry, the weather would undoubtedly worsen.

By the time the crew were pulling themselves aboard the lifeboat, the bustling cloud had already thickened overhead and a cold wind sprang up from the east, a woeful harbinger of rain. As the crew hurried efficiently about their various tasks, the boat's great diesel engines roared into life like a rudely awakened giant. As it was untied and readied to return to the slipway and safety, the impatient transfer boat bumped roughly against the lifeboat's deep blue hull. Even in the estuary there was a rapidly rising swell.

'Shore boat's away, Cox,' called the deck crew as the navigator took his place and prepared his sea charts for the journey.

'Standby to let go mooring!' Andrew eased the throttles forward to slacken the shackle tension.

'Free for'ard,' came the snappy reply above the strengthening wind. As the boat cleared the buoy and started out along the estuary, the mechanic busied himself with the radio. 'Coastguard, coastguard, coastguard, this is lifeboat *Dauntless II*, crew of six, now at sea and mobile to man over board, fishing vessel *Anne-Clare*, Anchor Rocks, over.'

It was a five mile run to the incident, a tough five miles that first took them out into the bay and then North to the rocky promontory called Anchor Point. An Atlantic ground swell added to wave heights, peaking around ten feet or more, limiting their speed to about fifteen knots. Maybe a twenty or thirty minute journey and every one of them a living hell for their friend lost at sea.

'*Anne-Clare, Anne-Clare, Anne-Clare*, this is the lifeboat, *Dauntless II*, at sea and on course for your last position, are you receiving, over?'

Meanwhile, the lifeboat left the relative calm of the estuary and began to hit the open sea beyond the sand bar. Andrew steered a course with port bow to the waves, it might lessen the crew's discomfort. Visibility was reduced by spray that topped the waves like the flowing manes of the sea's wild white horses. Wind beating against tide created over-falls and spindrift on the crests of deep green waves. A translucent deep green, a beautiful captivating colour that enticed, and commanded attention. Then came the eagerly awaited reply. *'Dauntless II, Dauntless II, Dauntless II,* this is the fishing vessel *Anne-Clare,* good to hear your voice. We have our fishing gear all aboard now, visibility poor and worsening. Bob Harkness went overboard about fifteen minutes ago. The only good news is that he was wearing foul-weather gear and life-jacket at the time. With only two of us left on board we are unable to search for him with any degree of safety.'

Most of the lifeboat crew knew Bob Harkness; a likeable young man with a family and many friends in the local community. Andrew spoke resolutely and quietly to his mechanic and navigator, 'Find his exact position now, then see what the current might have done with young Bob since their first call. Let Mark know, we won't let him down, soon be there,' then his keen eyes were back on the green and white of a wild and growing sea that stretched away into an uncertain future.

Meanwhile, old George Millar looked pensively out of his shop window at the changing sky, 'Just like today,' he mumbled, his thoughts far away. Head down and shuffling his weary feet slowly across the seemingly rolling floor boards, it might as well have been yesterday, it was all so clear to him. He leant forward to press his hands on the counter edge just as forty years before he'd pressed them on the storm soaked rail of the *Princess Dauntless.* 'Some fool in a cabin cruiser – no right to be out there! Idiot!' He paused from his brief anger and was aware of being back in his shop, the wind rattling the door as if to wake him from his recurring nightmare. But he was soon at sea again, raging green waves with spindrift that conspired to rob any lost souls of rescue. Eventually they'd come across the hapless small boat by sheer luck. She was starting to founder, rolling more and more, deeper and deeper. To all the crew, brave indeed as they were, it looked a certain lost cause. But Robert, their coxswain would have none of it, resolute he was, he would never give up, never. Neither could he bring himself to ask anyone to do what he wouldn't do himself. 'George,' he'd said, 'here, take the helm.' With George now at the controls, Robert made his way to the rail and, with an almost beyond human effort, boarded the stricken vessel. For a moment the crew saw his intense eyes and keen hands earnestly searching for any sign of life. Then suddenly that silly damned boat rolled hard on a wave and capsized. Not long after that, she slid bow first deep from sight.

George was overwhelmed by the haunting memories he'd carried alone for too many years, aware that he must finally tell what he knew, someone must hear his tale. 'Oh, we searched and we searched for our beloved coxswain until fuel and us was near exhausted. I swear on my life I saw him once, in a deep, fleeting trough, still wearing his sou'wester and high enough in the water to see his life vest. Oh, I shouted and pointed but it was only I could see him. He was waving us away - gesturing for us to leave him in that watery hell and go home. I'll never know the truth of it. His image haunts me to this day, a day just like this.

Some there were that praised him for his bravery and some there were that cursed him for the very same, leaving us like he did. His body was never found and to this day the sea still has him. Our dear Robert is still out there somewhere.'

Putting on his coat and hat, George Millar left the shop, locked the door and slowly made his way to a place he once knew so well, the lifeboat station by the old quayside. He tucked in his scarf, turned up his collar and wiped a tear from his eye with a worn sleeve. How could he ever forget?

'There she is, off the port bow,' came the lookout's cry, as the *Anne-Clare* came into sight. Andrew was decisive, 'Radio to Mark to hold his course and speed steady, we're coming close alongside, make ready the crew to move up to the flying bridge.' At the same time, he dropped a few revolutions off the powerful engines and deftly brought *Dauntless II* around to run parallel and on the windward side of the rolling fishing vessel. They were close enough to shout across and gather useful information, enough to initiate a search pattern that gave them at least some prospect of locating the lost fisherman.

High up from the lifeboat's flying bridge, all eyes scanned the chaos of a boiling sea. All were eager and ready to shout and point the moment they found young Bob.

Motoring on, above an insatiable deep, the valiant crew's rescue boat pitched and rolled steeply on a giant cloak of deep green as though Neptune himself was shaking it. At fifteen minutes gone, the navigator voiced his grave concerns, 'Look, Andrew, we've near enough completed the official designated search pattern and we're edging closer all the while to the sunken rocks off the Point. As we have wind over tide I think the current may have taken him closer to shore but the wind will have moved the *Anne-Clare* relatively further out to sea. We won't have much time.'

With time and tide in a deadly race against them, Andrew decided on a couple of sweeps closer inshore and nearer the treacherous submerged rocks off the Point, then failing that, they would be obliged to repeat the already unsuccessful standard search pattern.

It was not going well at all. Visibility was already appalling. Nothing found inshore, they began to motor seawards again, when suddenly Andrew caught a glimpse of someone in the water, he began to shout, 'We have him!' but went deathly quiet when he realised this was not their friend Bob. No, this man was older, wearing clothing from a bye-gone age . . . and under an old sou'wester, his face shared a knowing smile. The old man in the water was pointing insistently and resolutely towards the next wave. Then he was gone. Andrew said nothing about his vision to the crew. Regardless of the cold logic that would have ignored the apparition's instruction, his soul made him look where he'd been told. Sure enough, as they crested the next wave, there in the trough was the lost fisherman. The shout went up in preparation to gather him safely on board.

Poor Bob Harkness had been in the water for what seemed to him an eternity. Spray stinging his face, fingers numbed to useless, cold biting deep into the bones of his body - he did not expect to survive. He knew any chance of being found in such a chaotic sea was against all the odds, it was a risk they all accepted when they took such work. Pulling his knees up to conserve what little heat he had left, alone and afraid he waited for the end to come. His heart had already sunk nearly an hour before, when he'd tumbled overboard, watching helplessly as the *Anne-Clare* motored away into the waves without him. Now, finally he'd succumbed to a strange quietness - just waiting for the deep to swallow him up.

Bob was completely unaware of the lifeboat's presence and its gentle, beam-on approach from behind him. That is, until he thought he heard, 'Come on dopey, we haven't got all day you know.' To begin with he ignored the voice, for earlier he thought he'd already seen and heard things out there with him in the nearby sea. Somewhat unnerving it was. As his body sank into another wave trough, something told him he was not alone. Like an old friend's voice calling to him on the wind. Then the voice came again, only louder, 'Oi! Don't you want a lift home then Bob? You'll go all wrinkly if you stay out here much longer!'

A shivering Bob flailed his cold, tired arms and legs weakly to turn around. Thank you God; he was saved; smiling friendly faces, arms reaching out, and the rescue sling already in the water for him. Tonight he would dine with his wife and children about him and not with Davy Jones. Soon, secure on board and being treated for exposure, he smiled thankfully as he could feel the powerful diesel engines carrying them like a caring father would his small child, safely away from danger.

Still on emergency channel 16, the mechanic radioed their success to the coastguard and conveyed a welcome message to the fishing vessel.

Dauntless II, now making way with the tide, managed an easy seventeen knots. They were all going home; every single one of them.

Even as they moored *Dauntless II* to the deep channel buoy, the shore boat was alongside. Bob Harkness would be taken away first to a waiting ambulance and despite his emotional protestations, attend the County Hospital for the mandatory check up.

After closing down, checking fuel and securing the lifeboat, Andrew and his brave volunteers were also ferried ashore. As he walked into the station, the first man Andrew met was old George Millar, 'Hi Mr Millar, what brings you down here? You brought my groceries?'

'I had to come. It was a day just like this when we lost your grandfather. I never told anyone before,' he said gesturing Andrew away to one side for privacy, 'but I thought I saw him in the water that day you know, waving us away, I can still see him now, like as though he'll pop into my shop any day. . . He was never one to give up, and yet we came home safe without him, we left him behind, we lost him to the deep.'

'Never you mind Mr Millar, you're a special man yourself, we all think we see things in the sea, in fact I believe I saw him myself today. He showed me where to find our Bob Harkness when all seemed lost for certain. Funny, he looked just like my dad described, had a smile on his face too he did.

He never did give up did he? Perhaps his spirit is still out there looking for souls to save.' Andrew touched the old man's shoulder gently with a strong hand, 'Best we tell no one else though, eh Mr Millar, best we keep it to ourselves, or else they'll be locking us both up! I'll get out of this wet gear and walk back with you to the shop, collect my tea things.'

At last our old friend George finally understood the truth of the apparition he saw that fateful day so long ago. One lost soul was grief enough for the village to bear but an entire crew lost on a fool's errand would be a pointless tragedy. Robert's resolute and abiding spirit had urged him to take the crew safe home to live and serve again.

At long last George Millar's own soul could once more rest in peace.

He smiled and knew, 'There'll never be another day like this, no, never like this one.'

Barnstaple

That strange boy of hers.

The phone rang. It was eight thirty in the morning.

'Hello. Maureen Grey speaking.'

'Hi mum, it's me, Steph,' during a short pause Mrs Grey stifled a sigh – she could guess what was coming next, 'Bob is having one of his funny turns and I don't want him at school when he's like that. Can you look after him today? Please.'

'Oh, dear Stephanie, he's such a weird boy, you'd think at age twelve he'd have grown out of it by now. You should have had a daughter, much nicer than boys you know.'

'Yes mum, I know, I'll drop him off on my way to work and pick him up about five this evening. Thanks mum, thanks a lot.'

There was a click and then the phone hummed ominously in her hand. She was slightly confused as she didn't recall saying she would have that odd kid for a whole day.

She mumbled to herself, 'Well, if' he's coming he'd better behave himself and I'm not missing my coffee morning with the WI, so he can jolly well look after himself for a couple of hours.'

Twenty minutes later an impish looking boy with a far away stare was duly dropped off at his Gran's.

'You be good for Gran, Bobby. You do as you're told and no nonsense,' said Steph, as she pushed him past her mother into the hallway. And with a whispered aside to her, 'he's not weird mum, he's gifted,' Steph was on her way.

Later that morning.

'Right Robert, I'm off out for a while, er, important shopping to do. You can make yourself a sandwich and there are biscuits in the tin ... not too many mind ... I've counted them. You can find a book to read in the lounge. You be good and I might make fish fingers and chips for tea time. 'And she was gone.

About two o'clock she was back and immediately went in to the lounge to see what the horrible boy had been up to. 'Robert!' she balled, 'what have you been up to?' She'd seen her mother's old green glass ink bottle on her shiny polished table along with various bits of notepaper all filled no doubt with childish scribbling by her daughter's son. She snatched the ink bottle off the table, scoring the mahogany surface as she did so, 'now look what you've done.'

'I'm sorry gran, it just came over me that I needed to write a letter and I didn't think you'd mind me using that ink.'

Stupid boy,' she thought, 'that bottle had been as empty as his head for as many years as she could remember.' She gathered whatever was on the table and threw it in the back of the old writing cabinet, slamming the lid down with a flourish, weakening its hinges in the process. 'No chips for you my boy, you can sit in the back garden and wait for your mother.'

About a month later, and still mourning her loss, Steph was sorting out her late mother's belongings, clothes to the charity shop, furniture to auction and the house on the market. Her mother had been killed in a tragic accident while on her way to WI. The driver said that she hadn't looked either way at all but stomped out straight in front of his van as though she was on a mission. There was nothing he could do.

Steph started to look through the writing cabinet, there was her old grandmother's empty green ink bottle, and there was a letter in her grandmother's unmistakable handwriting. What was strange though was that the paper itself was quite new and the letter definitely not more than a few weeks old. It had been written with an old style nibbed pen and that powdery old black ink not available in the shops any more. Tears filled her eyes as she remembered her uncannily wise and thoughtful grandmother. Holding the paper in both hands, she read in a dumbfounded silence. The letter was addressed to her mother.

"My darling Maureen, I hope you will read this in time. Don't go to the WI next week, stay at home. Should you not heed this warning then I expect I'll be seeing you sooner than I'd hoped, God bless you, your loving mother in spirit, Victoria.'

The inexplicable and extraordinary letter from the past and the completely avoidable accident both remained a complete mystery.

They never did fully appreciate just how gifted that weird boy was.

Barnstaple

The Phone Call.

Phoebe was forty seven and now lived alone. She retired on ill health from a medical laboratory, her husband Robert having contracted a super bug that she'd inadvertently brought home from work. It was a sad case, there was nothing to be done, and even the best of antibiotics were ineffective. Two years later, Phoebe had moved away from the area to start a new life with an estate agent she'd met on line, but it hadn't worked out like she'd hoped.

So, Phoebe just made do with life as it was, with a very occasional visit back to see her mother in Rose Cottage retirement home. Recent events had further conspired against Phoebe, her car had proved unreliable and she was struggling to get the right medication for her depression, the lawn needed cutting, the local branch of her bank had closed and so had the nearest post office. Anything that needed doing was all down to her, no one else to help. Phoebe kept putting off visiting her mother, it was such a long way to travel and she wasn't even sure if her mother would know her anymore such was the rapid onset of dementia. 'Perhaps tomorrow,' she thought.

Tuesday evening and although it wasn't late, Phoebe felt exhausted and couldn't keep her eyes open. Not sure how long she'd been asleep, Phoebe was half woken by the faintest touch on her cheek, and her hand automatically brushed it away. Perhaps a spider or a fly, who cares, even though it seemed persistent she was tired and fell once more into a fitful sleep full of dismembered dreams.

Her mobile phone was to wake her again. In the darkness, she reached out for the luminous screen and pressed the green button. 'Hello?' she questioned drowsily.

Her mother's voice came clear and loud, hard to believe that she was some two hundred miles away. 'Hello Phoebe dear, I had a feeling you might visit soon, thought it would be nice to speak with you first, I don't want you worrying and going to lots of trouble.'

'Oh mum, how lovely to hear from you. Yes, I was thinking of tomorrow. You sound really well, just like your old self.'

In the darkness Phoebe's little bedside clock, quietly tick tocked its way past an unobserved midnight and more.

They chatted joyfully without any sense of place or time, until her mother finally said, 'okay my dear, time for me to go now, love you lots, you take care of yourself and no need to come all that way to visit, we have said it all over the phone. Love you always.'

The phone went dead.

Phoebe smiled, fluffed the pillow and slipped into a satisfying and long overdue slumber, not once pausing to wonder how her mum had obtained her new mobile number or why the staff at the home had allowed her to use the phone that late at night.

Nine fifteen, Wednesday morning and the house phone sounded its harsh call to action. Phoebe went downstairs to answer it.

'Mrs Phoebe Williams? Rose Cottage, duty nursing sister here, I'm afraid a have some bad news for you, you might want to sit down. . . your mother passed away gently in her sleep just after one this morning. The end must have been pain free and she had a most peaceful expression on her face. When you have taken it all in please call me back and we can discuss the necessary arrangements.'

Phoebe packed a small bag. Today was the day she'd visit her mother. She owed her that.

**

Bideford

The Torrington Road Gibbet.

It was Doreen's first time in Bideford, she'd come to visit her old pen pal Pamela, who lived in a little terraced cottage on the hill beyond the police station. They first met through a little known spiritual organisation, an ancient collective for those with interests in 'the other worldly'.

It was early September and a pleasant evening about an hour before sunset when the two friends took a stroll by the riverbank and out along the Torrington road.

"What a strange place this is, and, if I didn't know better, I'd be frightened," said Doreen.

"Well Dor, you're the one to know what's strange, what with your spirit dealings and all that. . . you've certainly always impressed me. . . I just don't know how you do it, I really don't," replied Pam, still wondering just what was so strange.

"Fancy you still having one of those awful things here," continued Doreen, pointing an accusing finger just down the road from the junction, "there, look, on the left of the road."

"I can't see anything Dor", said Pam peering over the top of her glasses and scouring the rising river mists for what strange thing could be out there.

Doreen didn't pause for breath, "Well, I'll go to the foot of our stairs if it isn't a gibbet of all things. . . awful things they were too. . . and something tells me this one has a story to tell. Come on, let's go closer." Pam was happy enough to go along with this suggestion, after all it was still close to town, it was still light and Doreen was obviously on a mission; Doreen could 'see' many a thing that ordinary folk could not.

"Pam. . . did once a highwayman ply his evil trade along this road?" inquired Doreen.

"Never heard of one Dor, not that I know of anyway", she replied slowly shaking her head in thought, then she went quiet as Doreen appeared to be listening to someone else.

"Is there anybody there?" Doreen asked calmly, "Please come closer. . . what is it you want?"

Though it was a calm and warm evening, Pam felt a cold breeze by her ankles and something soft brushed her face; she could hear nothing but Doreen's murmured conversation and the light rumble of traffic crossing the old Long Bridge in the distance. After twenty minutes or so, Doreen was back in the present. Turning towards town she said, "Come on Pamela, back to your house, and I'll tell you all. . . there's work for us to do here!"

They entered the house by the back door, "Go on. . . what did you find out, Dor?"

"Kettle on first Pam, then, pen and paper and we'll sit at the kitchen table. . . there is much to tell. . ."

"His name was Tom. Though not sure how old he was, he thinks he was an orphan. He was probably about twenty five years of age, a swarthy young man, scruffy and unkempt, with dark straggly hair. Locals called him 'Black Tom'. He'd been a runaway apprentice and could neither read nor write, something that no doubt contributed to his demise. He lived almost wild, surviving hand to mouth, begging from travellers on the Torrington road. Tom was befriended by the somewhat shrewd and outwardly benevolent landlord of an Inn, an Inn of ill repute some few miles between the two towns. Tom could often get a meal there for running errands or cleaning out the stables; sometimes he would sleep in them, despite the Inn being permeated by an apparent evil best avoided.

A blurry image came to me as he described the Inn, close by the river it was, a low, cob built building with a thatched roof, next to it leaned similarly built stables, there was a small carriage outside and about four or five horses, fine looking animals, not cart horses. Grey smoke came from a single chimney in the middle of the roof. I caught a glimpse of armed men running about, then the vision vanished into blackness and I found myself with Tom again, listening to his tale of woe. The Landlord was a powerfully built somewhat charismatic man called Rufus Hench, though that may not have been his real name."

Pamela nodded an acknowledgement of the name and promptly made some notes.

Doreen continued, "Rufus was very popular with travellers, always plying them generously with drink and meat and befriending them. In those far away days, many a traveller on that road would fall prey to some devious local highwayman and it wasn't unknown for a lone traveller never to finish their journey at all. The local magistrate and squire would often meet at the Inn to discuss their plans to catch this vicious local footpad.

Poor Tom still can't understand why it was him they beat, dragged away, tried and hanged. Rufus Hench had promised Tom he would put in a good word for him at the trial but in the event he did not turn up and in consequence Tom stood alone, illiterate and defenceless against his accusers. Poor Tom's body was displayed on the gibbet we saw, as a severe warning to any would be thieves that came that way. After the hanging, the robberies stopped."

Pamela finished making her notes and with an air of excitement proclaimed, "Tomorrow Doreen, we'll go to our town library and see what we can dig up, I know the lady in there, I'll phone first so she can better help us."

Later the next day, they climbed the few steps that entered the town library, "Hi Pam. . . and you must be Doreen, Pam's friend, welcome," said Rosey the reference librarian, "after your phone call I had a good search of our archives. . . not such good news I'm afraid, come on through to the back office and I'll show you what we have."

They gathered around the desk upon which various documents, old and new were scattered.

"Right", said Rosey, "the bad news. . . no record or even vague inference anywhere to an Inn on that road, no highwayman, no 'Black Tom' and no gibbet either and there's a reason for this. The good news is we have a lot on Rufus Hench. He was a very rich man who apparently came from London and commissioned a fine house to be built on the quay. According to the records we have he came to the town just before the civil war. He appears to have been very popular and generous and soon became not only Mayor but also Customs and Excise Officer, in which capacity he served benevolently for fourteen years until he emigrated taking his wealth with him; after that he seems to have disappeared completely from public life. Unfortunately there are very few records that survived from before Mayor Hench's time due to a fire only a few months after he was elected. Only the fire and any subsequent history remain on record. Sorry about that, perhaps your Tom the highwayman did exist, but now I'm afraid no one will ever know the truth."

"I suspect in our hearts we already knew the answer Pam," empathized Doreen as the pair left to walk soulfully up the High Street.

Perhaps one quiet day, if you're out along the Torrington Road as the mists are rising from the river you too might hear Black Tom's continuing plea for justice. . .

**

"And as a single leaf turns not yellow but with the silent knowledge of the whole tree,
So the wrong-doer cannot do wrong without the hidden will of you all."
Gibran (The Prophet)
**

Bideford, East the Water.

The Victorian Fireman's Axe.

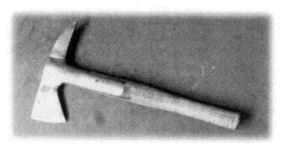

Events are told from the perspective of the axe itself, for who are we to say that the inanimate has no right to share its story?

We were such good comrades, that old fellow and me; constant and dependable companions; we'd been together for over thirty years; faced death and disaster many a time, side by side; the crumbling stairs, the choking acrid fumes; just a way of life for us both.

I suppose, in a way, we were both forged in fire. He was born around 1874 and I in 1892. We worked together in a small but industrious little estuary town. The tidal river ebbed and flowed carrying various cargoes for the warehouses not so far from our station and many a time the firemen would pick up a few 'silver darlings' for dinner from the herring fishers on the quay.

Though it wasn't a big station it saw many changes, even whilst I was there. The horses and 'steamer' were still there when I started, the place was heated by a coal fired boiler and there were various outbuildings storing hay and the like – I never went in there myself, had no need of me I suppose – but others told me how it was.

Though the place was somewhat frugal, it was clean. Twice daily the tile-red painted floor was washed and was clean enough to eat off; the brass work of door bell, steps, fire door mechanisms and all the equipment was so polished you could see to shave in – not that they did – many of the men had fine sets of whiskers. A row of polished brass helmets rested on hooks above smart, collarless double breasted tunics – the sort of tunic that inspired every man to stand tall and proud that ever felt its fit. It was with this tunic I would wait, waiting for the bells to go down and my comrade to come and fetch me.

For a few years, until he died of old age, a scruffy stray brown dog was adopted by the station. They used to laugh a lot at his antics, but admired greatly the dog's courage so close to fires; I think they called it 'Braidwood', though I cannot tell you why, but it did seem to amuse the firemen greatly. Anyway, that dog lived the life of Riley, well fed, slept by the boiler, and then, when the alarm sounded, would run out into the street and follow the men to the fire. What a life, what a lucky old thing, ah, how I envied that dog.

Where was I? Ah, yes, change. The station was to have the new electric light, and later, though the big brass hand bell still hung on its bracket, we were to have a big electric bell fitted. Every few years the station would be sent a new pumping appliance, (those on the outside, who I was informed knew nothing, called them fire engines). The old one would be zealously polished and cleaned with pride as it would be sent to a less busy station, and we had a reputation to honour. The new one would take its place and result in a flurry of activity, starting it up, stopping it, starting it up, pumping water, men running with hoses and ladders with lots of shouting going on from the watching white helmeted officers. My comrade never wanted to be one of those officers, it just wasn't for him, for he had a deep sense of duty which he felt was only truly satisfied at a place the men called, 'the sharp end'. For this I am eternally grateful as it's the only place I can work. He was good at what he did, come to think of it, so was I, we were a formidable team, us two.

Then, one day, he didn't come in to work; I was placed alongside some boots and on top of some folded uniform and fire tunics, then taken by the Brigade wagon to a place I later learned was called 'brigade stores'.

After all my valiant and unstinting service I was to be incarcerated, in a small dark room, in a box.

Occasionally the door would be opened and, along with the store man's hand, light would come in and bring a glint to polished and waiting steel. The hand would fumble then select from the box, and one of us would be taken. Sometimes the choice was rejected and the 'un-chosen one' was thrown at the back of the tiny wooden room, never to be allowed back with us in the box.

We, who had given so much to change other's destiny, were now uncertain of our own.

Sometimes, when this door was opened we could see young men in new uniforms, with buttons bright and thick black polished leather belts. One time, when the door was left open by accident, we saw one of our brothers, a chosen one, being handed to one of these keen smart young men. He grasped the ash handle and made some amateurish chopping action with the blade. It amused us - he would learn. He was only young and now he had one of us to look after him – to stop him sliding down a roof to his death, to open locks that barred his way, to quick release the pressure in a snaking hose dangerously out of control, oh, so many things our brother would show him. He put the axe in his belt, the cupboard door was closed. We were never to see either of them again.

It seemed forever that we stayed in that small wooden prison. When all was quiet outside and the store men home to bed we would share our stories …. of action, of noble strength and relentless courage; like our comrades we were prepared to do all that was required and to make sacrifice when duty beckoned. We often wondered why, when we had served so well, and given so much, what we had done to deserve a fate such as this. Strange, but one morning, about lunchtime, we overheard the store men discussing the state of an axe that had been returned much the worse for wear, chipped blade, scorched handle. Finally we heard, …….'If only they could talk, what stories they could tell us, …. ah, well, …… I'm afraid it's in the bin with you,' and so saying, the store man dropped our valiant brother into the rubbish.... Too bad the cry for mercy fell on deaf ears.

If only they knew of the stories that were being told, just a few feet away.

I well remember telling my brothers one cold night about the last shout I went on with my old comrade ……………..

It was a deadly dark and bitterly cold November night, a winter wind pattered sleet on the dormitory windows, it was the last of our twenty four hour duty shift and tomorrow would be a rest day. Then, in the small hours of the morning, the big six inch electric bells burst fearsomely into life. Men, driven by duty, habit and a shock of adrenalin leapt up from their beds, blankets cast aside and eyes wide staring open as they rushed for the rest of their fire fighting uniform.

They could smell the smoke filling the air as they prepared themselves to turn out, the driver strenuously hand cranking the petrol engine into life. Two more men pulled the thick ropes that unfolded the great red wooden doors of the appliance room and they looked into the winter street to see by the light of the engine's lamps a mixture of driving sleet and billowing thick, yellowed smoke.

They knew, tonight of all nights, this was a working job they had on their hands.

It wasn't far to go, just down the road at one of the old wharf buildings that backed on to the river.

It was a hotch potch of a building, part stone , part brick, that had been added to many times over the years, making a labyrinth of secret places the demon fire could sneak undetected to trap and cut off the unwary. It was a building of three floors and part basement, about one hundred yards deep and about thirty yards wide. It was used mainly for storage of mixed goods, almost anything could be there, wool, timber, grain, jute, anything; the fire seemed to be located on the second floor and was 'showing a light', flames being visible through breaking windows. The Sub Officer had himself and six men; he sent two of them quickly away to locate and set into a hydrant, the pump man stood by the controls. The Sub pointed and shouted his orders, "take a line of hose around to the windward side and play the jet through any windows on the second floor …. Break them if you need" ………. and two more men were gone, struggling with their heavy canvas hose into the dark. Now they were three, "Right," he said, trying to sound confident but deep down knowing this to be a daunting task, they would need the Angels with them tonight, "Come with me; we'll have a quick look inside. Bring a couple of lamps; let's go".

So close we were to the fire and so far we were from help, it would be twenty minutes at least before another crew might arrive, we were on our own.

The main door was padlocked against us, it was a job for me and I didn't hesitate, with my brave but aging comrade … a tough steel point through the hasp and a wrench of the ash handle and the lock was in two. Just as we took our first wary footsteps through the doorway one of the men from the hydrant reported in, out of breath, gasping, "Line in from hydrant, Sub, but jet's hardly reaching second floor!"

The town only had a two inch diameter water main and the pressure was never much good at the best of times. There were no ponds and any wells in the vicinity would not last a minute.

The Sub seemed to stare into the air as if looking for an answer, then, realising something must be done quickly or the fire might spread to other buildings, as sparks and glowing embers were already being carried in the wind, he made his choice, (as we too must make our choice in time), he shouted loud, above the roar of the fire now competing with the roar of the engine running nearby, "Right!" "Get the pump moved to a corner in case the building comes down, find any one in the street that can help and set into open water, get a second jet to work". As the man turned to leave, the Sub Officer shouted after him, "and take him with you, get going!" This left just the Sub Officer and us two. I think he kept my comrade with him for a couple of reasons, to save him from all that arduous, heavy work setting in to open water with that awful cumbersome rubber and wire suction hose, and secondly because of all the years of experience and knowledge that could prove invaluable inside this growing inferno.

"Come on," shouted the Sub, "let's find the stairs."

It wasn't long before we found them, they were made of stone, not good this, stone stairs had been known to collapse without warning; give us timber stairs any day, you knew where you were with them. The noise increased as we made our way ever upwards, so great was it that we didn't hear the call from below. "No water!" The tide was out, too much mud ………

They fell back to setting in to the hydrant, exhausted and covered in cold mud from their exertions to reach the water's edge. They had, however, improved their water supply by shipping another standpipe into a main a street away.

The crackling jet was now beginning to play through an open window, quickly turning to steam and occasionally hitting a glowing cast iron pillar, one of many that supported the floor above.

Sharp and very hot slates were now cracking and sliding off the roof to the ground below, tiny burnt holes sprung leaks in the canvas hose, the crew with the jet sheltered as best they could. They didn't know what else to do; they could only follow the last order. They waited amongst the falling debris for assistance to arrive or their Sub Officer to return.

"What a God forsaken mess," cursed the Sub officer, as we surveyed the stacked goods of the first floor. Timbers above creaked and the sound of falling slates and spalling stonework filled our ears, "If only we could salvage some of this ..... but... just the two of us ...." His voice trailed off, then, "what the hell was that?" The Sub stared at us disbelievingly. We had heard it too. It was a scream, almost inhuman in nature. "For God's sake," the Sub gasped, "there's someone up there; what the hell are they doing here?"

"Night watchman, that'll be my guess Sub," said my comrade in a calm but urgent manner, "it'll be old Fred, he's got a gammy leg .... that's why they gave him this job. .... I'm pretty sure I can find him Sub."

"Go for it then, take care, you damn well come back safe; I'll check on what's happening outside and get help in to you as soon as it's possible," with that said, the Sub Officer's big, dirty hand patted him admiringly on the shoulder and in an instant he had melted away down the dark stairs to the ground floor.

I had a moment to reflect on this ... what did my comrade mean, '**I'm** pretty sure **I** can find him', what happened to the '**we**', after all we wouldn't have even got this far without my help. Then I realised I'd fallen into the old ego trap, I'd forgotten that what endeared us most to the Brigade was adherence to our motto, '*Undying service without praise,*' it brought us the greatest of respect and status. We asked for nothing but to be allowed to serve, we were almost invincible.

We found the next stairs, now of timber, and had to brave a small fire on our way upwards.

I tell you, I remember thinking, 'I hope he knows what he's doing!'
Frantically, and beginning to choke in that killing air, we searched for old Fred; we found an open window and looked out and down, there in a crumpled heap on the flag stones below lay the reason for the scream, it was indeed old Fred. Just out from the window to the right was an old cast iron rainwater down-pipe, when young and fit it is easily possible to climb down such as this if you know how. Perhaps Fred had considered this his only way out; it was a young man's game that, even for us it looked decidedly dangerous, and we'd done it before. We turned to leave but that demon fire had sprung its trap and spawned destruction and chaos behind us; now it was we that must find another way out!

Water sprayed in through a broken window on the far side; with plaster off the walls in places, timbers creaking and bits of broken slate peppering the floor we made our way across, at least there some fresh air came in. My dear comrade gulped in some clean air then called out to the men below. At first they could not hear him but then they did, almost everything was dropped as they rushed to retrieve the wooden ladder, ... we could hear the orders snapping out apace, we knew they would be here soon .... 'Head away ... extend.... well ... lower.... under run .... heel to building ..'

A panting, red and whiskered face suddenly appeared at the window. .... "Bloody bars!"   ..... "Bloody barred windows!" .... "Give us yer axe 'ere and I'll try and break one free!" I was quickly passed out through the broken glass into the slippery new hands still numb from the soaking cold of holding hose and branch.

I fell; clonk, clonk, clonk as I hit the rounds of the ladder on the way down, accompanied by an anxious cry of 'stand from under!' I heard the heavy fire boots thumping down the ladder ... 'pawls, step out!' screamed the now shocked and solitary fireman footing the ladder, then I was passed from hand to hand and we returned to the head of the ladder, at first he shouted out to my brave comrade that all would be well, that we were back and he wasn't alone anymore. Using my chisel shaped spike our whiskered rescuer hacked at the stone work that held the bar in place. There was no voice from inside, there was no sign from inside ....I wondered if he had gone back to try the drainpipe ..... all we could see from outside was the deep red glow of a big fire in a slow rolling sea of choking dark smoke, then it happened .... Whether it was the roof that gave in or the hot gases had ignited – suddenly all hell broke loose and searing hot gas and flames appeared at every window with a loud but dull 'crump'. The fireman on the ladder was forced to duck down and away from the window to save himself. He climbed quickly down shouting, "get some water in through that window – quick – for God's sake ......"

The Sub Officer turned up, extra crews had arrived, water supplies had been improved and progress was being made.

My comrade? I don't know, I heard others talking .... 'he must have found another way out' ....and another say, 'yeah, if any one could, he could. I wouldn't be surprised to see him come out that front door any minute.'

I didn't hear or see any more as the initial crew were relieved and sent back to station and I with them. They made a pot of tea, opened the door of the boiler and stared silently, with both hands clutched around hot mugs, drying their wet clothes, at a fire that was now not their enemy but their friend. I remember thinking, as we warmed up safe in our station, 'I pray he's alright.'

Dawn was beginning to break and a new day commence.

Well you know the rest, I can't imagine anything bad happened to my comrade, if it had I should have been with him, much guilt remains in my heart that I didn't stay with him, if only I hadn't slipped... but I just can't think that, it's too much to bear.

I've been many places since first being forged in fire and I can still do today what I could do one hundred years ago given the chance. I spent many wasted years lost and alone in various cupboards, but for the last ten I've been an ornament on a shelf in a retired fireman's home – I don't think his wife likes me …. hang on … here she comes now   … with that damned duster and polish …..must stop now … got to go … thanks for listening to me, not many give me the chance you know … .. if only they would …. that's all we ever needed ….. just a chance ……that's all…

**

*"It is not because things are difficult that
we do not dare.
It is because we do not dare that
they are difficult."*

**

Bideford - the new bridge.

Well met, on a bridge to the other side.

A fading summer Sun had hushed the
land to sleep. High up on the old bridge that
spanned the tributary, a clumsily dressed, thin
young man in his early thirties stood wide
awake in stillness. Transfixed like a rabbit
caught in headlights; eyes captivated by the

swirling torrent far below; a torrent that rushed on unquestioningly in its blind search for the ocean's dark but welcoming shroud. By two in the morning all was graveyard silent and he was still there lost in thought, the air was warm and his frayed T shirt and old trousers were all he needed that night, or any night . . . his body and soul braced forlorn on the wrong side of the railings.

Suddenly, a voice shattered the silence and with it went any peace he might have had. The young man nearly jumped out of his skin, for he'd not seen or heard a soul for three hours or more. 'Steady on mate,' said the voice, 'didn't mean to make you jump.' The young man gripped the railings even more tightly with both hands, pulling his back firm against the bars, his mind now in turmoil, for he'd hoped to end it all alone.

There was something of an Aussie twang to the voice from the dark; its owner came closer, stopped a few feet away, rested his folded arms on the parapet and continued talking as though finding a walker, never mind an erstwhile jumper, on the bridge at this God forsaken hour was quite a normal occurrence.

'So, what you doing here then, young fellah? Sure is a lovely night and what a beautiful view you've got yourself here. Betcha that river's full of life down there, them crabs and fishes don't sleep at night yer know.'

The young man didn't know what to say, in fact he didn't want to say anything; he just wanted this bloke to clear off to whence he came. He'd been content with his prior misery. However, curiosity had the better of him and he sensed a non judgmental calm from his surprise visitor, 'Crumbs, you made me jump, no pun intended, what on earth are you doing here at this hour?'

'Well young fellah, I could ask you the same, but me, I'm what you might call of no fixed abode, a gentleman of the road, homeless if you like. It's not so bad you understand, though it was before, loads of things went wrong before, lost the missus and kids, parents died, injured at work ... in the army I was you know. Oh they paid me off all right but money was no compensation nor cure for my ills back then.'

'So what brings you to this road, this bridge, tonight then?' the apprentice jumper asked again.

'Oh, dunno really, just going with feelings, always follow the good feelings I say. When you walk with a smile on your face you'll always get some coming back your way. It just felt right to go further south, more rural, nicer people; chance of a few jobs on a farm or something. Food in the hedgerows, berries and the like – yeah, that's about it really – just feelings and as it was a warm night I thought I'd take advantage of the cooler air and quiet road. Then I met you, nature watching from your fine perch on my bridge.'

'Sorry about that,' said the reticent jumper, who somehow felt empathy for the ex-soldier and his losses in life. He realised that somewhere, way back, we're all linked together somehow. In fact, this happy tramp had suffered far more than he ever had himself, 'You never thought of ending it all then?' he enquired.

'Yeah mate, I thought about it but when I got there some young fellah had nicked my spot – you gonna be long?' the jovial tramp's smile could just be made out in the moonlight.

For some peculiar reason, perhaps contagion, it appeared funny to the would-be jumper and he smiled back, 'Oh yeah, good one, very droll,' he said. The strange thing was, the thoughts that drove his racked body to the bridge were changing and as the thoughts changed so did his feelings. In fact, the tramp was right, it was a beautiful view, it was a great night, the moon smiled down on a land at peace with itself and he, for that moment felt part of that. What had possessed him to ever want to throw such beauty away? 'I'm coming back over,' said the reformed jumper.

'No mate, stay there, you'll be fine, in fact, I'll join you over there – that little bit of fear, the adrenalin rush just spices life up a bit at times, makes you feel more alive than ever – come on, shift over a bit, give us a hand.'

The pair of them nattered away for ages, like two long lost pals reunited. Interspersed with tales from down under, of joys and woes, the gentleman of the road implanted his wisdom and set the seeds of hope and resolution in his young friend's mind; he'd given him a gentle push – in the right direction. Good thoughts began to bring the young man good feelings and they filled his very soul and body.

'Well, I reckon I'll thank you kindly for all your help and wisdom and be on my way home now, for tomorrow I have much to begin.' So saying, the young man clambered roadside of the railings, his body and spirit lightened from the burdens he'd earlier carried to the bridge. Now it was as though he'd dropped them into the swirling depths below to be lost forever. He was now free and felt it, like somehow he'd paid off some long outstanding debt at last.

'So long mate, I'm gonna stay a while longer, before I make my way to the other side.

You be good, you think happy, feel happy, and don't waste yer life …live it well.'

As the young, now rehabilitated, jumper reached the end of the bridge he suddenly realised he didn't even know his saviour's name, he turned and started to shout his question but there was no point in finishing the sentence, the kindly stranger had already gone. 'Oh well,' he thought, 'After his good deed tonight I hope at last he finds somewhere to rest in peace, he's obviously decided not to wait any longer on the bridge after all.'

That young man went home, made a better life, repaid that good deed a thousand times over and never forgot his friend the tramp, well met on the bridge to the other side. He resolved to share his story with anyone who would listen, just like he had listened that fateful night so many years ago.

And now you have heard it. I must leave you, for there are others waiting in the darkness, on bridges they built for themselves.

If you would only look, you will find joy on every path.

No matter how dark it seems.

**

'After the long slumber of ignorance, a single word can change a man forever.' **Nan Guo Zi**
**

Challacombe - the moor.

Still Happy Children of Exmoor's Past.

I followed the old gent outside and a short distance along the moorland track. He seemed to be unsure of his footing, as though confused or dizzy. 'You alright old chap?' I asked.

I'm afraid I startled him, but for an old man well in his eighties, he turned quickly, his expression, one of bewilderment.

'I'll have to sit down a minute,' he replied quietly, 'I think I'm having a bit of a funny turn.'

I watched as he slowly lowered himself to rest on a dry grass bank. There was a light wind at his back and the weak warmth of a September sun on his face. He peered with aging eyes directly at me, as though trying to recognise me from somewhere in his past. 'I just had a most weird experience.' Staring at a now empty moor, he began, 'I've just been in an old thatched Inn over there, well, at least I thought I had. I was tired from walking and went in to see if I could have a drink and rest a while. Typical of a country pub, they all went silent when I walked in. All dressed in the simple clothing of working peasants they were. Then they carried on, completely ignoring me. They just stared past me, like I wasn't there. I thought for a moment the landlord had definitely seen me, then his gaze changed and he looked right through me and continued to serve others first. Damned ill mannered I reckon. In my day we were taught to be polite to strangers. Anyway, I'm standing there in a fog of tobacco and wood smoke, being ignored like I'm invisible for God's sake, when two young children appeared from nowhere and ran through the bar. Now, they did notice me and looked me straight in the eyes, so they did, then at each other, giggled and off they ran again, happy as can be. There seemed to be something different about them from the others, like they had a knowing about them, and I reckon they were the only ones who could see me. They came by twice more, each time stopping to stare in curiosity, and off they'd go again, laughing excitedly. Well, I didn't feel like hanging about such an unwelcoming place like that, so I upped and left. I was just coming to terms with it, when you walked up behind me from nowhere and spoke.'

As with a frail hand, the old gent shielded his eyes from the lowering Sun, I heard the bell ring for time being called back in the Inn. Without further ado I went back inside, back to tend the bar in the Fox and Goose Inn. An Inn cursed long ago by the fatal fire that razed it to the ground, September 1867.

The old gent continued to rest and ponder, now quite alone on an empty moor, adjacent the crossroads and a scattering of moss covered stones. His eyes softly closed against the weak warmth of a still bright September sun. The gently fading sound of children's laughter was replaced by the whispering of the west wind at his back.

I evermore tend the bar at the Fox and Goose but so far the old gent has never come back to see us again.

**

Combe Martin

Hangman's Hill.
Great Hangman Hill, North Devon,
autumn of 2012.

Young Henry Challacombe was a very happy and much envied man in the pretty coastal village of Combe Martin. Henry had just inherited the 'house of dreams', a quaint cottage tucked away in the seclusion of a wooded valley below Great Hangman Hill. He was a local lad, as his surname Challacombe foretells. His family was inextricably historically linked to rural Devon, never having left it and in distant times a family not without power and influence in those parts. Henry was a down to earth, hard working soul with a great love for the coast and moors, their mysterious ancient ways and indeed their intriguing secrets too.

A building had stood on the cottage site for more than four hundred years and although the garden was heavily overgrown and Foxglove Cottage as it was known, was in need of restoration, there was an inherent quietness about the place; something rare and beyond price. Despite ivy creeping in around the old casement windows, there was nothing he felt he could not achieve; such was Henry's enthusiasm for life.

Henry's overwhelming joy was completely entwined with the new love of his life, his soul mate, best friend and soon bride to be, Annika Larson. Coming from a reclusive community in the east of Sweden, she was twenty three and just two years younger than Henry. Annika Larson was more than the stereotypical pretty blonde who'd caught the eye of all men who ever met her, she was also admired by the local women for her poise, welcoming smile and something much more profound, which only intuition could appreciate, she possessed the presence of something spiritual, something of the eternal knowing that only exists in a special quietness. Perhaps it was an esoteric wisdom inherited from her shamanic Scandinavian ancestors.

Henry and Annika worked tirelessly but happily on renovating their new home. It was a happiness that seemed destined for eternity such was the almost unbreakable bond between them. Sometimes on a summer's evening, Annika would cook a delightful Swedish meal in the garden over an open fire, while being amused by Henry's attempts to entertain her with his second hand guitar; somewhat in the early stages of being mastered. But those seemingly timeless days slipped by unnoticed and were marked only by shopping, collecting building materials or occasional visitors who had actually managed to find the cottage.

By early autumn they were preparing for winter, nothing like a Swedish winter of course, but winter none the less. Fruit from the overgrown orchard was selected and put to store, potatoes were dug and bagged in the lean to shed and the log store stacked with fuel for their wood burning stove. All was looking as good as it could ever be.

On the last day of September Henry said something he would no doubt regret for years to come. But how was he to know? How could he?

"Come on Annika, we'll have a day off, a well deserved day off with no jobs to do. We'll take some lunch with us and spend the day up on the big hill and watch the seabirds over the cliffs."

Annika smiled, 'What a lovely idea, we live so close to the hill but have never been up there yet, I'm looking forward to it. Something tells me it will be exciting . . . I just have a sort of premonition. Yes, if anything, I now realise the hill has been calling to me all the while. How strange.'

Henry nodded with a wide smile of amused admiration and fetched his walking boots from the cupboard, picking up a warm jacket too. . . just in case the fine day clouded over. They took a slow and comfortable walk, hand in hand where the way permitted, though at times the path would dictate they walked alone. As they left the wooded valley behind, the hill of bracken and gorse rose up steeply in front of them. They paused and looked back, the cottage was now well out of sight and their attention again turned to reaching the clear grassy summit. 'I know it's nothing compared to your Swedish cliffs Annika but this hill has the highest sea cliff in all England, an impressive drop to the water and dangerous rocks below. I've seen it from a friend's boat.'

Henry was revelling in the climb; somehow being on the hill gave him a surreal sense of power. It almost felt like it was his hill and he owned all he could see.

As they closed on the trig point cairn, Henry thought for a brief moment they might not be alone, he was sure he'd glimpsed others in front but now they were gone. He dismissed the foolish thought as there was only him and Annika, the way he hoped it would be forever. Henry lowered his rucksack and looking contentedly seaward, sat down with his back to the cairn. He smiled and looked up at his lovely wife to be. She looked happy as she too gazed seaward, her long blonde hair lifted lightly by the sunny breeze. Henry imagined her ancestors looking seawards just as she, watching for the Viking long ships to come home safe at last from some frightful adventure. He sighed, Annika was unlike anyone he'd ever met before, she was truly special.

Annika's face abruptly changed, as though bewildered by something. Then she spoke vacantly as if simply repeating what another had just whispered in her ear, *'Stora Odin får dem att sluta. Odin för syndens skull rädda oss,'* she said.

Suddenly, as if realising what had just happened, Annika's pretty face twisted in horror and she slumped to her knees next to Henry.

'Something terrible happened here Henry, we must go home, now, I cannot stay here a moment longer, help me please, help me, I want to go home, now please. Henry threw the rucksack over his shoulders and helped Annika to her feet, he had never seen her like this, he'd never seen her unhappy nor ill in any way before and now this. It was a worryingly long trek back down the hill as Henry struggled to support the weakening Annika. A rumble of thunder from over the great hill signified a change in the weather.

He redoubled his efforts and they entered the safety of their cottage just as the heavens opened and a brief but fierce squall beat hard at the doors and windows.

'Thank the gods, we weren't caught out in this storm as well,' thought Henry, 'that's all we'd need.'

It had turned cold with the rain so Henry lit a small fire in the stove and, forgetting he'd already a hot drink in his flask, put the kettle on to boil. He sat Annika down by the warming fire, kneeling in front of her and looking full of care at her worried face, 'What is it Annika? What on earth happened up there, is everything okay?'

Annika stared intently at the flickering flames, 'Her name is Freyja Larson, curiously the same surname as mine. She's dead. She was on that hill that dark day of devil's days in September 1657. I am the first person since then that has enough knowing to hear her spirit and can speak her language.'

Henry stood, fetched a warm drink and placed it in Annika's hands, then knelt again, looking into her eyes, desperately trying to find the old happy Annika he'd known earlier that very day.

'What was it you said to me in Swedish up on the hill? He asked quietly.

'Oh, it was what Freyja had called out in her anguish at the fatal moment. She had implored Odin to make them stop, she pleaded to Odin for pity's sake to save him. Obviously it did no good, he was still hanged.'

'Hanged? Who was hanged? How do you know anyone was hanged?' begged a worried Henry. This was completely out of his league, he knew nothing about such things, all he cared about was Annika and their life together. It was everything to him.

With the drink held cupped in both hands now growing cold and the fire slowly dying, Annika told Freyja's story and of the awful apparition she'd seen on the hill that day.

"It was long ago at a time when foreign blood was only welcomed when spilled on the battlefields of Europe. Freyja was a strong, pretty young woman, saved from a shipwreck by a local fisherman who fell in love with her, and she with him. There was a childish feud that she couldn't quite understand, between her brave young man and the local lord of the manor. The lord took advantage of his position as local magistrate and falsely accused the young man with the unlikely crime of poaching. Though completely innocent, he was hastily found guilty and sentenced to hang publicly and his body be left on a gibbet on the great hill for all to see.

Freyja was treated with great suspicion by the local people, they didn't understand her and she was shunned. If anything, they also feared her, even the magistrate avoided her attending his court. She would never survive long in the village without the young man who had once saved her life from the sea. There was a crowd on the hill to witness the sentence carried out and their unbecoming barbaric cheering drowned out Freyja's desperate call to Odin. As soon as she was alone on the hill, she cut him down and in her desperation to be with him in death, dragged him with the greatest of difficulty to the cliff edge. There, she held his lifeless body in a warm embrace and tumbled over the edge. She hoped that on the jagged tide washed rocks below they would forever be united in death and live new and happy lives in Asgard, the land of the gods. But just like her call to Odin went unanswered, her dreams too were washed away by the waves that had once spared her life. Her soul has been trapped on that cursed hill for an eternity."

Henry rose slowly to his feet, put another log on the fire and went thoughtfully to the kettle again. It was still light outside and the rain had long stopped. As he looked out of the window he noticed smears of mud on the glass. 'Where on Earth did that all come from?' he said aloud to himself.

Annika answered. 'It's Freyja; she's trying to get in.'

Then with a far off look in her eyes, 'Jag måste gå hem.'

It was one of the few phrases that Henry understood, 'I must go home.' His heart sank like a stone. He knew now that it was not so much Annika's wish but it was Freyja that had finally found a way to go home.

Great Hangman Hill, earlier known as Hanged Man's Hill, is bare today, no trees, no gibbet, just grass and the distant memories of life's mysteries, secrets and tragedies that flourish about the moors and coasts of North Devon.

Old Foxglove Cottage still remains, with its neglected garden overgrown once more and ivy creeping in through the gaps in the windows.

Of course, the villagers had missed the happy young couple and gossip was rife in the shops and inns as regards Annika's sudden and mysterious disappearance. A lonely and despondent Henry did remain at the cottage for the winter but it is believed he too eventually slipped away quietly for Scandinavia to try and find his love again.

We can only hope he did, but sometimes hope is the only remnant of once noble dreams.

If the gods will allow it so, they will surely meet again, how can we endure otherwise?

Perhaps tonight you might be kind enough to offer a prayer to the gods for them.

Spare one too, for the soul of that pitiless magistrate of 1657,

  His name? . . .

Henry Challacombe Esq.,

Freyja

**

Countisbury

Mo's Dream.

It had been a tragic and frankly awful six months for Maureen, or Mo as her few close friends knew her. Mo's mother had died suddenly and without any prior warning only the day before Mo and her good husband, Alan, were to pay her a visit. Mo was a kindly lady in her early forties, same age as Alan, and the death of her mother at only sixty two, was an unwelcome and devastating shock.

Mo was a precious only child and her steadfastly protective mum had always looked out for her well being until they'd moved many miles away for Alan to find better employment. The joy of visiting, laden with gifts, photos and news to share, took a crushing blow when the neighbours explained what had happened.

When they entered her mum's house it was neat and tidy, even more so than normal. The best china tea set was laid out ready on the polished front room table. Sharing the table was an old shoe box containing her mum's 'little treasures', her grandmother's wedding ring, her father's military medals, lots of photos of Mo as a child and a miscellany of buttons, tickets and postcards. There too, lay a writing pad opened ready on the first page; alongside, a simple but pleasing silver fountain pen, a gift from Mo, with black ink and broad nib; however, the page was blank, not a mark, just blank. Alan and Mo often wondered what the empty page would have told them. If only they had gone the day before, if only her mum had written the note, if only, if only. . .

Following this sad event, Alan was kept busy with his work and Mo with sorting her mum's estate, of which she was the sole and meagre beneficiary; her mother had been as poor in material possessions as she had been rich in emotional and spiritual matters.

Mo had many sleepless nights, thinking, dreaming, worrying, grieving and every night questioning just what the letter would have said. Who was it to? Why didn't her mum start it? Why was she writing it and why was the little 'box of treasures' alongside? Were they connected?

Sleep came and went but the questions were always there, even in her dreams the questions came.

Mo even thought about visiting a medium or psychic or anybody that might be able to fill in the gaps. Mo kept putting it off though because Alan wasn't much of a believer in such strange goings on.

Then, one Thursday evening in September, on his return from work, Alan told her, "Right Mo, that's it, get your bags packed and dig your walking boots out of the under stairs cupboard. We are off on a little holiday."

"Oh, that's a lovely thought Al, it really is," she replied warmly, "but I don't think I'm up to it. . . and you have work tomorrow. . . "

"Nope! Got the day off. . . and Monday too. . . we're going and that's that. It will do you good. . . get away from this place and feel some fresh sea air, eat some good country food and maybe take a few walks on the moors too," said Alan confidently as he held his head up high and smiled a smile of satisfaction.

"Moors?" Mo enquired, "Where are we going then?"

"Never you mind, it's a mystery, no, it's a surprise. Everything is booked, all taken care of, already paid for, you'll like it, you'll see. So, sort out your gear and we're off at the crack of dawn. . . OK, perhaps not quite that early. . .

and we'll buy a nice breakfast somewhere on the way."

So it was to be, and on one fine early September Friday they arrived at Countisbury; it was about noon when Alan pulled into a large car park to the sound of city tyres on country stones.

"Here we are Mo, we have arrived. . . our new home for the next three nights," announced an excited Alan, "let's grab our bags and register at the Inn then the afternoon is ours." Mo was temporarily excited too, she had forgotten all her troubles. . . just for a while that is. Alan saw her mood change quickly as Mo noticed the old church and graveyard beyond the car park, her thoughts returning to her mum and the letter she never wrote. "Come on, that's enough of that, old girl, this is a lovely happy place, somewhere new that we've not seen before, it will be a lovely holiday. Let's see what they have for lunch. . . anything you want you can have."
Mo snapped out of her thoughts, "of course, I'm sorry Al, I should be more thoughtful of you too. Let's treat ourselves; you can have a steak if you like." So saying she threw her rucksack over one shoulder, picked up her handbag and they crossed briskly over the deserted roadway to the Inn.

It was a warm reception that welcomed them to their new 'home'. They settled into their upstairs room, situated above a quiet part of the building and with fine views of open countryside and a blue sky decorated with small white clouds. "There, look at that," said Alan, "if God were to paint a picture then surely it would look like this. Come on, change of plan, let's have a light lunch and get out there amongst that lovely nature."

"OK, love, I'll catch you up, I just want to lay here for a moment and enjoy the peace and quiet after the journey," murmured Mo as she kicked her shoes off and reclined on the bed, her eyes almost closing as if to enjoy the peace the more.

"Don't be too long. . . " replied Alan as he quietly closed the latched door behind him and softly descended the stairs to the bar area. The ground floor of the Inn was huge, very long with changes of levels and room widths; it looked to Alan as though it may have been extended or altered many times; it added to the charm, it added mystery. Alan soon made friends and chatted to a couple of pleasant local characters in the bar downstairs. Meanwhile, upstairs, as though someone who loved her had sent it as a gift, a gentle sleep overcame Mo. . . and almost as quickly she was visited by a strange dream. It was as though she had gone back in time and was sitting in a quiet corner of the Inn downstairs; the only light, the light of early morning, came in through some cobwebby windows to her right, wood smoke drifted from the open fire along an oak beamed ceiling and a smiling, plump faced, pretty girl in servants garb walked happily towards her from the far end of the long room; she was only a few feet away when the sound of a wagon and horses on the old earth and stone road outside reverberated through the Inn as though it really were there; It woke Mo with a start. Now wide awake she listened intently to an unexpected and all pervading silence then glanced at her watch; she hurriedly slipped on her shoes and went in search of Alan.

"Ah, there you are love, the landlady has made us some sandwiches and suggested a fine short walk to the headland where we can eat them and look across the sea to Wales. How's that?" said a beaming Alan.

Mo began, "I've just had a strange dream. . ."

She was quickly interrupted by Alan, "come on Mo, we've had enough of dreams for a while, we're on holiday, let's enjoy our time here. . ." and so saying picked up the neatly wrapped sandwiches and taking Mo by the arm led her to the Inn door and the bright outside world of a September Devon. Alan was going to do his utmost to help Mo out of the doldrums of the last six months; this was going to be a special holiday.

They walked through the churchyard and out to the headland. The landlady was right, it was a beautiful spot. They were blessed with warm sunshine, found a comfortable rock to sit on and were sheltered from a light breeze by a bank of gorse which still carried its alluring coconut scent. The sandwiches were excellent and time just seemed to disappear, being replaced by contentment. As the sunshine began to fade their thoughts turned back to the warm Inn and its open fire. "Al, let's look around the church on the way back, I'd like that," she said, standing and stretching her arms with pleasure.

"OK," Alan replied, adding, "we'll have a night in by the fire, there's a nice one in a back room, with settees by it, we'll have a meal and why not a few drinks. . . we'll just chill out and enjoy our time. . . Right, the church it is. . ."

As they walked quietly alongside the outer wall of the churchyard towards the little wooden gate, Mo had a flashback to her earlier dream, a little shiver ran down her spine, she put it down to the cooling air and didn't mention it to Alan, he didn't seem to want to know these things. They spent a while reading the gravestones and wondering at the disparity of lifespan, there were those who made their eighties and some who never saw their first year out. "Disease, probably," intimated Alan, "simple diseases we can treat now, were killers then. How lucky we are to know all what we do these days."

That evening they enjoyed a lovely meal, found one of the Inn's many quiet and secluded corners and played some of the board games the Inn kept for guests. They played until Alan realised that perhaps he wasn't used to drinking so much and started losing the plot as well as the games. "I'm off to bed love," slurred Alan knocking his legs against the low table they had been using.

"OK dear, I'll be up shortly, I might see if I can get a hot chocolate," Mo replied.

When Mo returned from the bar with her hot chocolate she was surprised to see another guest sitting there, a pleasant old lady with a motherly look to her. "Oh, I'm sorry," said Mo turning to go.

"You do no such thing my dear, you sit ee here, I be Grace Elworthy and I'm not one to turn you away," Grace gestured reassuringly and smiled warmly.

Taking a seat opposite, Mo said considerately, "I should leave you in peace really."

"Ar, dear, we're all looking to find that," Grace replied softly.

"I'm sure I've heard that name before somewhere," quizzed Mo.

"'tis an old name round these parts, perhaps someone in the Inn mentioned it," suggested Grace.

It was the beginning of a long and heartfelt conversation during which Mo told her all about her mum, the letter, Alan's work and how he was treating her to this special holiday.

"What a dear old soul," thought Mo as she later climbed the stairs to bed, "I feel so much better now."

Later that night Mo had the dream again, she saw the same girl with the mop cap walking towards her from the far end of the long room. . . it seemed she walked with real purpose but still smiling happily. . . then something quite strange happened, Mo became the girl in the dream; it was most odd, there were times when she felt that she was awake enough to tell herself it was a dream. . . most odd, most real, she felt awake, the dream world and the waking world seemed in confusion. Mo, now the servant girl, actually felt herself opening the Inn door, a different door to the one she knew as Mo the guest, she stepped outside and down two steps onto an earth and stone roadway. It was early morning in the dream and to her right, in front of a small barn and stable, was a young man preparing horses for a wagon. He had harness in hand but none the less lifted his cap and smiled coyly at her. . . Mo felt herself responding, this young man was the love of her life.

Up to then Mo hadn't taken notice of the iron pot she was carrying but now she did, for it slipped heavily from her hand and clattered loudly on the stones where it fell. The horses were spooked, they became increasingly more skittish and the young man struggled to calm them, he couldn't hold them both and one made off, bolting straight down the road and directly at Mo. Mo was frozen with fear, transfixed to the spot, the sound of hooves and the desperate cries of the young man filled her ears all in a distorted slow time. The last thing she heard was the horse's frenzied breath and the last thing she saw was the sky vanishing into blackness. Mo sat bolt upright in bed with sweat pouring from her brow, her body surging with adrenalin, her breathing rapid and her hands trembling. Mo turned to Alan to wake him. . . tell him all about it. Mo stopped, looked at Alan snoring peacefully and resolved she would keep this silly dream to herself. Poor Alan had had so much grief since her mum died, he deserved this special holiday and he certainly didn't deserve being woken up at three in the morning by his crazy wife.

It was well over an hour before Mo slept again, there were no more such dreams. Still, she was up early in the morning and with questions to ask. She pulled the duvet around her sleeping Alan's shoulders and quietly crept downstairs in search of breakfast. . . and some answers too.

Mo was too early for breakfast so she found a quiet corner in which to think on the nightmare of last night. She was so lost in thought Mo didn't notice her new found friend and confidante, the little old lady Grace, join her at the table. "Good morning, dear," said Grace quietly.

"Oh, hello Grace. . . not sure it's all that good mind you. . . I had a nightmare last night. . . saw a young lady die in an accident with a horse. . . right outside that door it was. . . brrr. . .," shuddered Mo.

"Don't you worry about things like that dear, all such things can be explained, I've not been about all these years without taking an interest in such matters. . ." Grace paused for a moment, and then continued, "I'll tell you all about it later, I think I hear your husband coming and you should enjoy each other's company without some old lady hanging around with you. Look for me when you have some quiet time and I'll tell you all." Grace stood quietly with ease and left. Mo was just thinking how well Grace walked for an old lady of her age when. . . "Morning Mo, crikey, what a night that was. . . I shan't be drinking as much today. . . how did you sleep?. . . come on, I think breakfast is ready through the back room. . ." Alan pointed animatedly in the direction of breakfast and gestured with the other hand for Mo to join him.

Alan and Mo sat opposite each other at the pine table, breakfast was brought in by the landlord himself, he placed the plates gently and asked if there was anything else. "No, we're fine, thanks ," said Alan. The landlord turned to leave, "No, wait a minute please," said Mo, holding her knife and fork at the ready, can I ask you a question?" The landlord nodded thoughtfully and Mo continued, "Tell me, do you have ghosts here? Do you know anything about a young woman, probably a servant who was killed by a horse outside your very door?"

The landlord smiled and said, "Ghosts? I can't say as I've seen any here, we've been here a few years now. Sometimes the locals speak of such things but I think the spirits are mainly in the bottles or in the customers. . . mind you, occasionally I'll hear the odd noise. . . but that's to be expected with an old creaky building like this one. . . even the wind howls by the door frame when it blows from the north," he paused and thoughtfully put his hand under his chin, then continued, "I have done lots of research on the building and its occupants and never come across any death of a young woman. . . I mustn't keep you; your breakfast will get cold." He bowed his head slightly, turned and left for the kitchen.

Alan hadn't been listening that intently but asked, "Wow, what was that all about then?" Mo didn't want to disturb Alan about her dream; he needed this holiday probably more than she.

"Oh, nothing really love, I just get the feeling that we are not alone here sometimes."

"You're right, we're not," said Alan sternly, we're being watched as we speak. This was most unusual for Alan to take such things so seriously and it surprised Mo, even startled her a little. Alan continued, "See, over there? I see eyes; watching us from by the doorway?" Mo hardly dared to turn her head to look. "I reckon he's after one of these sausages!" Alan laughed and was back to his normal self as Mo turned to see the big black dog who lived at the Inn staring intently not at her but at the table and its contents.

She had to laugh herself, she needed to lighten up, she'd made something out of nothing. . . time to forget it and finish breakfast. "What shall we do today then Al," Mo smiled, "take that dog for a walk?" They both laughed. . . it was a special holiday after all.

"There's a lovely old lady called Grace who's staying here, you must meet her sometime, she's a real angel, great to chat to about life," confided Mo.

"Yes, there are some wonderful people around here. I was chatting with a couple of locals at the bar and they told me that there's a spectacular geological fault called the Valley of the Rocks. They told me how to get there and that it was worth the effort. . . but not to miss the Sunday lunchtime here. . . they said the Inn is renowned for its excellent Sunday lunches, they said there are people who come twenty miles just for the dinner. I do just love a Sunday roast," said Alan looking wistfully into the future. . . almost certainly at a Sunday lunch.

"OK, Valley of the Rocks, here we come. We'll go soon and walk off the breakfast before you restock with lunch. I sometimes wonder if anything else but food occupies your mind. Come on, teeth cleaned and boots on, let's be having you," she chuckled to herself, threw her paper napkin remonstratively onto her empty plate and went to prepare herself for the next adventure.

The couple enjoyed a bracing walk in the Valley of the Rocks. It was a little colder than they expected as much of the path didn't see the Sun until afternoon. None the less it was exhilarating and they took a few photos of Castle Rock and the odd wild goat or two to take home for the album. They were pleased to return to the warmth of the Inn and even more pleased with the roast dinner. As the Sunday lunchtime diners started to thin out and go home, Alan and Mo enjoyed a few drinks and chatted with a local farmer and his wife. God, life was good on holiday, if not quite so good for farming; hedge cutting, ploughing and storing the winter feed, all needed doing. Alan enjoyed hearing of the practicalities of life on the moors. . . and enjoyed the fact they weren't his to worry about. . . God, life was good on holiday. As the last of the customers left the Inn for home, the tables were cleared and wiped by staff before they too disappeared into the kitchen. Suddenly all was quiet as the grave and Alan was struck by a bout of tiredness, "must have been all that talk of work on the farm," he told Mo.

"More like that big dinner and the few drinks that followed," laughed Mo, "why don't you go and lie down for a bit, I'll stay down here and read a while. . . I've seen a nice book on short stories about somewhere; it has a nice red cover with a table, a candle and a letter, looks interesting. Off you go, I'm fine."

Good as the book might be it was not why Mo wanted to stay in the bar, she hoped that Grace might still be at the Inn; Mo had noticed that Grace wasn't one for crowds; in fact she'd noticed that Grace even avoided Alan, despite Mo desperately wanting him to meet her. As Mo searched and rounded one of the quiet corners of the long room she almost bumped into Grace coming the other way, "Oh, hello," they both said in unison just like twins.

"Well, my dear, now there's no one about to listen to our conversation so I reckons I can tell you what you wanted to know. Let's sit by the inglenook, it be warmer there for ee. No one will come back in the bar until later this afternoon. They have their own dinners now and forty winks after," said Grace with a wink of her own. "About your dreams; they were more than dreams. . . sometimes they are you know. . . I sense I can tell you these things; it is your time to know. You saw the girl, well young woman really, because you were seeking something beyond your own living world. Your mind was open and receptive, that's how she could share with you her own experiences. It happened long ago, she was an orphan, only known by the name of Hannah. In fact she was about twenty three or four when she was killed, not so long before she was due to marry. I reckon that would be about 1892.

 As you said, she was chubby faced, happy girl with a great purpose in life; she never fulfilled it and her spirit stays here trying to complete that something that can never be.

The stable lad never stopped loving her and he never married another. . . he's buried over in the churchyard across the road, though not near Hannah; she was a pauper you see and buried in common ground with no marker. He has a grave marker, even if it is much worn and hard to find now but his spirit was content with what he had done in life with his sacrifice and dedication to Hannah, so his spirit has moved on. Your mum has moved on too, she was content with life, she could see you were happy and that was her purpose in life, just to see her daughter happy. I think this holiday was as much her idea as it was Alan's. He was suddenly inspired to act. . . a seed was planted in his mind and his heart answered. I also think that seeing Hannah is also a message just for you. . . many might feel her presence but precious few will ever see her as you have done. . . It's a message that tells you there is somewhere else to go beyond death. Those who have fulfilled their purpose in life simply move on and those that have yet to do so struggle to find a way to join them. In consequence they can relive their demise over and over, trying to find a way of atonement, trying to find redemption, a way out of the spiritual prison their own mind has created.

I also think that Hannah had a message for you too. . . about being happy. Hannah didn't question about her parents life or death, she lived her orphan life as best she could, as happy as she could. For all her problems she was a happy girl. There's the answer you seek, be happy. It is what your mother would have written had she the time. Your mum sent you this message, this special holiday, today of all days you can be happy again. I've said too much I'm sure, I must leave you now to think. . . and smile. . . I must go; I have other things to attend to now. Perhaps I'll see you before you leave."

Mo so wanted to hug that dear little old motherly lady that had befriended her so kindly but it didn't seem appropriate at the time, she'd catch her later. Mo was at peace, the peace she had sought for months. With a smile on her face and a skip in her step she went in search of Alan. . . wake him and take him out for a walk to clear the cobwebs. . . or perhaps just quietly lay down beside him and sleep a happy dreamless sleep.

Come Monday afternoon the car was running well, almost as though it knew it was on the way home and the Autumn Sun shone brightly all around. The road was quiet, the car was quiet and Alan drove slowly so as to enjoy the experience, he felt good, all was well with the world, a beautiful world. Deep wooded combes gave way to undulating hills and views of the Somerset levels; he took the view in like taking a long and welcome breath.

"That was a great little holiday, wasn't it Mo," said Alan rhetorically, "and we didn't think once about your mum's letter either; I wonder what she would have written."

Mo reached out and touched his hand, "sometimes there are no answers; sometimes you don't need the questions either; we might never know but our soul will." She smiled a contented smile and looked out of the window to enjoy the rest of her journey; as she did so, her mind wandered back to the last few minutes at the Inn. . . Alan was carrying their bags out to the car when Mo looked for Grace one more time, she was not to be found in all her usual haunts but Mo did find the landlord checking the bar stock, "thank you so much for a wonderful holiday," she'd said, "can you tell me where I can find Grace, she helped me so much and I want to say goodbye."

"Grace?" enquired the landlord, always willing to help if he could.

"Yes, that's her, Grace Elworthy, lovely old lady that's been staying here for the last few days."

The landlord had put down the dust cloth and bottle, slowly turned with a puzzled look on his face to look Mo in the eyes and said, "But Maureen, you and Alan were our only guests this weekend, no one else is staying here."

**

*"No argument is so convincing as is the
evidence of your own eyes."*
**

Dartmoor, not far from Princetown

The Portal

*A tale about a group of spiritualists
who take it just one step too far.*

It was agreed; they had three months to
prepare for a journey of a lifetime.

The seven ladies were part of a spiritualist
circle, which met once a month in search of
enlightenment and they had an exciting new
plan; a plan for the summer solstice like no
other. Well, no other that had been practised
for several hundred years for sure.

'I have developed a meditation plan which we
all must follow to the letter. Each of us must
be proficient in connecting with both the path
and with each other in order for it to work.'
They were all on the edge of their seats as
Hazel explained further. 'The old manuscript
found in a Dartmoor barn some hundred and
twenty years ago and left to me by my dear

late aunt has been transcribed by the archivist at Truro records office. Along with the map, we are told all we need to know about opening the portal, the gateway, to the other side. I cannot emphasise how important it is to practise our collective meditation and develop our discipline to the highest order. Now, Jill has something to tell you. Jill, please.'

Jill stood with ease from her seat and spoke of the practicalities. She was a keen hill walker, which suited her for the task of guiding all of them safely across some difficult, remote and rarely visited territory. '*Breus Entrans*, is the old Cornish name, it's not on ordnance survey but is on the manuscript map. Old wives' tales say it is known as Doom Tor and it boasts a group of minor standing stones, seven in all. Once again there are no modern records of this stone circle, possibly because it is notoriously awkward to reach and archaeologists have plenty more important sites that offer easier access.'

Jill looked around the room, everybody was engrossed; this was going to be the culmination of a magical and life changing journey they had sworn to take. Hazel nodded encouragingly at Jill. Jill continued, 'seven of us, seven stones and the seventh hour. . .' a murmur around the room was quieted by a serious frown. . . 'Yes ladies, seven in the morning. We need to be there and ready at the seventh hour. I have arranged B&B for all of us together, about 6 miles from the site. We'll need an early night and a very early start. Here's a list of suggested, better think compulsory, items you'll need to wear and take. The weather should be okay but we won't risk it. A dry spring will mean the mire in *Breus Golans* should be passable with minimal risk. So please, all pray for no rain, ladies.'

They all worked hard to prepare for the journey, a journey both physical and spiritual. They hired a minibus for the 20th June and met at Hazel's house with all the stuff they needed. The weather was perfect as they set out for the B&B, a delightful and remote farmhouse run by a psychic animal healer and her farmer husband. Extra camp beds had been placed in as many rooms as possible to accommodate the chattering excited group of soul seekers. They all enjoyed an evening meal of carefully chosen foods, some picked from the moors, some from the farm garden and generously provided by the hosts. They had all agreed to no alcohol, much to some disappointments. Still, they were definitely on a high without a drop of the hard stuff. Except for Maggie, at 35 the youngest of the group, she'd smuggled a bottle of vanilla flavoured gin along with some cheap doughnuts in her rucksack. Maggie was ever the rebel.

'We're up at 5, girls, so no chatting all night. Chamomile tea and then we turn in for a good rest so we can make the most of this rarest of opportunities to view the great portal of eternity.' Hazel looked around the room until she received a nod from each of the group.

There would be no signal up on the moor so Mary took advantage of the farm's satellite connection to update her social media – until about two in the morning. Time just flew, it was so absorbing, like going through a time portal itself. She wasn't aware of her body or time as she silently tapped out her important messages into the ether.

Just as bad were Patsy and Jenny, who were sharing a room together. They always had plenty to say and that's what they did most of the night. They weren't tired at all, the excitement of the trip, the food, the farm and it's psychic occupant, the plan to see the great spirit gate . . . all these things served to keep them quietly engrossed. While they gossiped, dawn was stealthily creeping closer to the eastern moors.

For all the ladies, whether they'd slept much or not, it still came as a surprise as doors were knocked and a lively voice called, 'Up ladies, time for breakfast. Come on, up and at it, come on, no dilly dallying.' Jill was relishing her position as walk leader; it reminded her of her youth and the army cadets she'd joined - just for the fun of it.

Bleary eyed and not looking like they were fully conscious, except for Hazel and the now indomitable Jill, they sat around the farmhouse table in unusual silence, holding their mugs of herbal tea.

Hazel tapped her mug with the spoon and the room went even quieter. 'Solstice time is five am but our appointment with destiny is at seven am. The manuscript explains the delay as being akin to a high tide following the full moon and not arriving simultaneously. We have two and a bit hours to turn up at the stones; Jill tells me that the last part of the trek is across pathless moorland and we must be extremely careful where we put our feet. There is no mobile phone signal out on the moor so any trouble is going to be all ours to sort out. Still, that's how it was for the ancients and in part it may raise our own awareness levels to advantage. We will see. Now, Jill has a few words to say.'

They all looked to Jill. 'We have about four miles of reasonably easy going, old farm tracks and the like, before we take on the open trackless moor. I suggest we keep as quiet as possible, keep the talking to a minimum. Once we reach the pathless section I would like everyone in single file. Each person places their foot in the exact place of the previous footstep. You will find this way of travelling very meditative in its own right and it is the way of the ancient tribes whereby an unknown number of people only ever left one set of footprints. For us there are added benefits, one, the leader, me, will be finding the best route from experience and two, you'll like this one, any tics waiting for a feed will be on me, not you!'

For some it brought a smile, from others a look of horror, they hadn't considered tics, bogs and the potential for death, they'd had a rose tinted image of a grassy walk in the sunshine like going on a summer picnic. Soon they would be tested. Today they would all be tested.

Shortly after and suitably attired, they gathered in the farm yard and with lots of smiles and 'see you soons' to the farmer and his wife, they set off with the slowly rising

Sun at their backs, their long shadows rushing ahead of them keen to reach the stones first.

'Not so sure we'll be seeing them all again, got a funny feeling about this,' said the thoughtful psychic to her husband.

He joked with her, 'you worry too much, you've never been right yet. Come on, we've work to do before they're all back having discovered nothing but blisters and tics and desperate for their dinners.'

Jill had been so right about the absorbing and meditative effect of walking in silence in a single line; Each concentrating on the previous footstep, like looking into the future but a future that was safe because your friend had already been there. Even Maggie was able to keep the faith, despite her shorter legs and plumper physique, 'heavy bones,' she always told others, 'just heavy bones.' Hazel stayed at the back, lost in thought for the untested ritual ahead; such was the terrible responsibility that began dawning on her.

The small hill of *Breus Entrans* was set in a shallow, bracken and grass filled valley. However, the prevailing wind had thankfully kept vegetation to a minimum on its summit. The stones were smaller than they had anticipated but there they were - all seven in a perfect circle and a gap or entrance where the eighth would have perfected the pattern. The group maintained their silence and walking in line until they were right next to the stones themselves. The Sun was higher now and already warming to their backs. It took Hazel a while to tear herself out of the silence which now firmly gripped her and the others, 'Well done Jill, that was truly awesome, I've never experienced such a feeling before, well done you. Ladies, please take your places on the inside of the circle and in front of a stone. Rucksacks and stuff from your pockets all to be left outside the circle. Start with Jill on the left of the entrance, then Jenny, Patsy and Maggie - in the order we practised at the hall. I shall be on the last stone by the gap. We have ten minutes left before the witching hour.' An expression Hazel was immediately sorry she had used, 'why on earth did I say that?' she scolded herself.

They took their places at the stones, each facing the centre of the circle where they imagined the portal must be. Beyond the centre each had a friend and a stone opposite, all but one, who faced the empty space where the eighth stone presumably once may have been.

The light breeze stopped lifeless, sound fell silent, only Hazel's soft tones could be heard, before they too would fall into the unknown abyss of space and time.

'Eyes closed and down, hands on centre, imagine finding the path that leads to the underworld, follow the path until you find a gateway, when we all reach that gateway we will feel the connection between us and see and feel the ring of energy we create in this sacred place. Remember, do not step through the portal that appears, just look to see what is on the other side and later we will share what we saw. Let us begin with a gentle chant for seven breaths, then seven silent breaths as we set out on the hallowed path. Let us begin. . . .'

Though some of the ladies were imbued with greater skills, their connectivity after the tribal walk had strengthened their bond enormously and it was not long before they were all deep in meditative state. Each unthinking mind became the observer of the external, of that not born of thought at all; each not knowing or caring what the other was seeing. As they struggled to complete the circle across the gap of the eighth stone, they saw a shape appear, human in frame yet without definition, more like a fuzzy grey aura. The figure, or what ever it was, completed the circle just as the seventh hour took its place in the enduring passing of the ages. The sensations were electrifying but none could awaken, so deep had they travelled into the underworld of their own imaginings. It was only afterwards that they would come to understand that each and every one had seen the same thing – in precise detail.

At this point all normal vision or interpretation of images was lost, the figures and the stones melded into the same indeterminable but present grey shapes. A shape began to cross the circle, across to the eighth place and the waiting grey entity. The two shapes left the circle together and disappeared. So that was where the portal to the other side had been and yet none of the ladies had been able to see through to the other side as planned. As suddenly as the shapes vanished, the spell of the sacred place was broken and the ladies were out of the dream world, back in real time to hear the endings of what to most of them was best described like a fading wail, not dissimilar to the last note of a wolf howling. Then silence, before the breeze blew again off the moors and the sunshine warmed their bodies.

Eyes wide open in the bright sunshine they each looked directly across at their partners, all except for Maggie, as it was her that was opposite the gateway. Maggie's slumped body was resting against her stone.

'Oh God no,' moaned Hazel, 'she's fainted.'

'Or been supping her gin,' said another.

'Come on,' ordered Jill. Being the first aider and guide on the moors, she had a pang of guilt about their joking, 'give me a hand to check her out.'

Jill knew as soon as she touched Maggie's arm that she had not fainted, she was dead. 'Quick, we need to lay her flat . . . come on Hazel help me, the rest of you stand back out of the way.'

In stunned silence they stood back as Jill desperately attempted to bring Maggie back with emergency resuscitation. Jill knew in her heart of hearts it was a waste of time but it was her accepted duty to try . . . even if it was for the benefit of the group to know at least they tried.

Hazel spoke quietly to Jill, 'It's no use Jill, she's gone. We need to think of getting off the moor now. Take the fittest of the group straight back to the farm, inform the authorities, the rest of us will cover her up and stay by her side until help comes.'

Jill reluctantly agreed and set off with three others as quickly as the ground would allow.

Three hours later, the sound of a helicopter filled the air, finally whining to a halt as it landed some two hundred yards away.

Paramedics confirmed the situation, strongly suspecting a heart condition after the overweight patient had trekked over such wild moorland and they explained what was happening. Maggie's body would be flown to the hospital for a doctor's signature and to maintain some dignity for the deceased. The remainder of the group was to be picked up by the moors rescue team, probably by Landover within the hour.

The rest is just detail.

After a very bumpy drive back to the farm house, they all spent a couple of hours consoling each other around the kitchen table.

The coroner's verdict was death by misadventure caused by a presumed heart attack following a strenuous and isolated walk on the moors.

Though each of the ladies suspected differently, they kept to the coroner's version. After all, who would believe otherwise? They had businesses to run and lives to lead that depended upon credibility. But they would always know deep down that what they saw was indeed real, Maggie's soul had crossed to the other side before her time, she'd always been a rebel.

Hazel was never to speak to others of her own deep insights, born of that fateful day - that the aura is a visible manifestation of life force, the soul does not reside within the brain but is symbiotic with aura. Usually the energy takes three days to leave a body on death; death being the permanent departure of the aura. Hazel considered that perhaps shamans and yogis experienced out of body events while their auras temporarily went walk about, but in Maggie's case, her spirit or soul was called by the gatekeeper to pass through to the other side and her life force left in the twinkling of an eye, visibly crossing the stone circle to enter the portal to eternity. Hazel knew that she could never share this awareness with others, as it flew in the face of the beliefs of so many influential and self involved people. It remains her uncomfortable secret to this day.

In the vain hope that her spirit will join their circle once more, every solstice the group still remember their friend Maggie, just as every solstice her soul joins countless ancients at the *Breus* stone circle to watch the Sun rise and to pray for a reincarnation that may never arrive.

Postscript:-
Breus - judgement   entrans – gateway   golans – valley
Many an old wives' tale has an ancient truth, Doom Tor was surely no misnomer.

A copy of the manuscript still occupies a place in the archives at Truro, my advice is, leave it there.

**

Exeter

The Ouija Board – Hannah's Tale.

It was coming to the end of another pleasant lunch time at the local council office canteen, Dr Joseph Dewar placed his near empty cup quietly on the saucer and looked across at his old friend Bob Rathbone; they'd been close friends since studying history together at Cambridge many years before. Glancing about him to see who might be in earshot, Dr Dewar confided, "There you have it then Bob, it's an old basement still in a structurally safe condition, probably covered over since the Blitz, the developers will be filling it in very shortly but as you know we are obliged to give it the archaeological once over before they can continue. Well, we did and we've finished with it. I carried out the investigation myself and if I can feel the energy down there then sure as hell you will too. It would make a terrific place for a séance and as long as you can keep hush-hush about it, I can provide you with access this weekend . . . Sunday is best, we don't want the politically correct health and safety mob snooping around. The nature of your interests doesn't exactly enamour you to the establishment."

Bob smiled the smile of the eternally grateful, "Joe, that would be brilliant, truly terrific, I have some new people interested in the spiritual arts, this is an opportunity sent from heaven. I'll make arrangements for us to meet up at the venue on Sunday, say about ten in the morning?"

Dr Dewar simply nodded his head in agreement.

The scene for the grand séance was now set. Bob Rathbone, professional psychic and erstwhile pursuer of all things strange and supernatural was soon back in his home and busy with the telephone, organising participants and swearing them to the most binding of secrecy. They were all told where and when they should meet and that Bob was especially intending to use the Ouija board. Access would already have been left open for them on the Sunday morning by his friend Dr Dewar. They knew it was going to be special event for they could sense the excitement in Bob's voice . . . plus it was all hush-hush, a really secret meeting, one to get the blood itself tingling. . . no one would ever know what was going on underground that day; it would be a case of out of sight, out of mind.

Sunday came apace.

Before the others arrived, Hannah, her cold and fear already overcome, was waiting on the bottom brick steps of the basement. It seemed like she had waited an eternity and she had long wondered if any one was ever coming. Then she heard them arrive, she heard their eager voices with offers of help; help to carry Bob's folding chairs and little card table, so useful for such events. The dim light in the basement darkened completely as the little group of spirit seekers blotted out the light of day at the basement entrance and very carefully filed down the shadowy brick steps.

Hannah stood and moved carefully to one side.

Soon, the candle lit table was surrounded by six occupied chairs.

"Okay, good, we're all here, glad you could make it. I hope you've all kept your promise of secrecy. We are some of a very few privileged people to be in this room since the blitz of some seventy years ago. Please make yourself as comfortable as possible; we don't want to fidget about once we start. Those of you who are new to this just relax and follow along with open minds. I don't anticipate that we will be incarcerated here in the darkness for too long, perhaps a couple of hours at most," explained Bob in his calm almost hypnotic voice, then with a grand flourish he took out his much loved antique Ouija board and placed it reverently on the dark green baize of the table. There was a veritable quiver of excitement; a truly tangible presence in the air. Next Bob took the planchette or pointer from his pocket; it was wrapped in a piece of well worn black velvet. "Now this," Bob continued, "is really something special, this heart shaped planchette is made from wood I salvaged from Bethany Street Church after it burned down the other year. It's the first time I've used it in the presence of others. . . I have a good feeling all should go well today and we will soon contact any spirits present".

Hannah was fascinated by it all, she had a strange feeling that this event was always meant to be, a sort of destiny; she felt like it was a chance to expurgate her demons and in some way perhaps find the spiritual freedom she had past been denied. For Hannah, this Ouija board signified a prospect of almost breathtaking proportions. It was an invitation she could not turn down.

While everyone else sat quietly, their minds filled with anticipation, excitement and not a little trepidation too, Bob's soft voice reached out to the group and into the encompassing darkness, "there are a few things I'd like to tell the new people before we start. If we do contact spirits, then it is often said that they are usually spirits of a lower plane. Spirits confused about how to move on, murders, suicides and the like, when the victim's spirit was never given time to accept and adapt. At body death, such a spirit may create an emotional bond with their immediate surroundings, perhaps like this basement. It is a little like the imprinting of new-borns on the first animal they contact in their new surroundings. There are many who say that what we do is all fake, you need to be aware of this scepticism and be extra careful about what you share with others. . . to be sure they will *not* understand. You must make up your own mind based on experience. Seriously now; what we are about to do is open a doorway to abnormal dimensions. The board itself cannot harm you, however, your own mind may. This is true in any walk of life but when it exposes your innate centre to possibly quite frightening and inexplicable experiences it can haunt you for the rest of your life."

The situation in the basement became serious and to more than one of them it seemed a little colder than when they first came in; a cool breeze had sprung up that had touched their faces like passing cobwebs. Bob took a small piece of dried sage and lit it from one of two candles. As his hand fanned the smouldering ember's perfumed smoke around the table, he asked that the spirits allow this place to be clean and good.

If it didn't affect any spirits, it certainly gave great comfort to the waiting group.

"Now please," said Bob in a firm and positive tone, "all those in the group who wish to join in, place your finger on the planchette, otherwise just remain still and calm and watch. Those joining in may ask their own simple questions, keeping them positive and not expecting any long answers."

Just four of the group chose to place their fingers on the board's heart shaped pointer.

Bob spoke first, "we come with truly compassionate hearts seeking to contact the spirit world. . . is there anyone here?"

After a brief pause, the pointer seemed to move all of its own accord to *'yes'*. Somebody in the group gasped; the following all pervading grave like silence filled only with the pounding of their own heartbeats.

Hannah sat quietly just observing, absolutely calm, simply spellbound by the whole event unfolding before her; She began to imagine that the séance was especially for her, and her alone.

Next, a young man called Finley nervously asked, "Was this your home?"
He was disappointed when the pointer did not move but Bob intervened and encouraged Finley again, "it's not moved Finley because the spirit is repeating the 'yes', well done."

"Are you a man?" asked Betty, a sixty something stalwart of the psychic group. The pointer moved leisurely but surely to 'no'.

Finley couldn't wait to ask again, "what's your name please?"
It took some time to spell it out as the pointer moved purposely but slowly to the letters, as

if the spirit was old, frail or just thoughtful . . .
'H' 'A' 'N' . . . 'N' 'A' 'H' . . .

Nobody spoke a word and the silence took on a perceptibly eerie quality.

Hannah thought deeply and privately to herself, "why, that's my name, how amazing, what a strange coincidence. I wonder what will happen next."

Bob took over, "Hannah, thank you for showing we are not alone down here, we are indebted for your contact. May I ask when you passed to spirit?"

'1' '9' '4' '2' came the clear response.
"That's a long time ago Hannah, were you affected by the war that was happening at that time?"

The pointer moved much more rapidly and instantly to 'yes'.

Bob picked up on the sense of agitation and angst that his question had caused but he continued cautiously, asking several questions that related to Hannah's life during the Second World War on the home front. The spirit seemed desperate to answer, almost

 seeming to be impatiently waiting, waiting for the next question to come, just waiting; forever waiting.

The candles were half burned down by now and Bob

was feeling hungry and thought the others may be too, he had also noticed a couple in the group shivering with cold on occasions, "okay, group, it is time we left Hannah in peace, we will once again thank her spirit for being with us, we will clean the board again with burning sage and we will meet at my house Tuesday evening to discuss our experiences. Thank you all, thank you Hannah and goodbye."

With that said and done, the group picked up their chairs and climbed the brick stairs, once again dimming the basement to obscurity as they themselves breathed fresh air and escaped the all pervading darkness they left behind.

Monday saw the ever impatient developer's bulldozers and diggers move in to do what they do best, flatten things. The basement was filled in and levelled over. Soon concrete sealed the darkness forever and work began on the new council car park.

Subsequently, during Tuesday lunchtime, Bob met again with his friend Dr Dewar, senior county archaeologist, at the council office canteen.

As Bob smiled the smile of the eternally grateful, he confided, "terrific visit

Joe, so good of you to think of me, can't thank you enough, amazing place and atmosphere. We managed to reach a spirit called Hannah, such a pretty evocative name, more unusual these days, I've not heard it spoken in a long while. . . anyway it would seem that she lived at that address and died in 1942, something to do with the war. All six of us had a wonderful time, regulars like Finley and Betty told me it was one of the best ever and it was a first-rate introduction to the three newcomers, Rowena, Mike and Vanessa, absolutely superb it was."

Dr Joseph Dewar leaned forward and slid a brown paper file across the table, "Bob", he said in half whisper, "I did the archaeological investigation myself as you may recall me saying, I neglected to tell you that we actually recovered unidentified skeletal human remains from the premises."

The file cover read,

Archaeology Dept
Ref 3021,
Basement
Old Calcutta Road Development

Bob expectantly opened the file and glanced at a few drawings, notes and photographs which he quickly recognised as Hannah's basement. One photo specifically caught his eye, the location of the skeleton . . .

slumped about the bottom two steps of the brick stairs.

Dr Dewar continued his analytical revelation, "An elderly female, height about five feet four, probably in her early to mid eighties, some signs of rickets and arthritis but otherwise no trauma. It is my considered opinion that she lived alone and was trapped and left in the basement following an officially recorded air raid on that area in, as you so rightly said, 1942. I tried the records office to confirm occupancy during that period but no relevant documents have survived intact. I think the poor soul starved to death or less likely asphyxiated while trapped in the basement. . . it must have seemed like one terrifying time without end to her. Chances are that no one knew she was there and the basement was well hidden with rubble, which is why it has only come to light recently with the building works going on. From our available evidence, there was no way I could formally identify the remains."

Bob Rathbone, professional psychic and erstwhile pursuer of all things strange and supernatural, reflected with a new understanding upon events, sensitively he shut the file and slid it back across the table, nodding sympathetically.

Dr Joseph Dewar, archaeologist and forensic scientist, took a pen from his inside jacket pocket and deftly wrote on the file cover,

'HANNAH'S BASEMENT –

FILE CLOSED.'

Author's note: I can tell you no more, for I too am sworn to secrecy. . . and perhaps I have already said too much. . .

**

*"If you don't keep quiet,
you will never hear the echo."*

**

Exmoor, near to Doone Valley

The Walker's Rest.

*(A stranger's brief tale of his life altering discovery
while out on the moors)*

Dave Baker, ever the friendly,
dedicated and conscientious man, was now
embarked on a life-changing adventure of
great significance. He'd only just emerged
from a reluctant and unhappy divorce and at
age forty three had also been made redundant
from his long term employment.

Now, with nothing and no one to hold
him back and with just sufficient money in his
pocket for a simple life, he decided to pack a
rucksack and see some of the world, well, the
world of nature anyway. To this end on one
fine and sunny September day he found
himself walking the high moors.

Not even sure of the day of the week,
Dave surmised it might actually be a Saturday,
but truth to tell, along with most of his

belongings, track of time had gone significantly astray.

He'd been walking remote parts of the moors for a few days by now and his down-to-earth clothes were somewhat in need of a good wash, as indeed was he. A respectable cooked dinner wouldn't go amiss either under the circumstances.

As the warmth of the day began to diminish and the omen of dusk foretell its reality, he started to walk more purposefully down a long slope into what appeared to be a lifeless but never the less curiously alluring valley. It wasn't long before rough heather under his boots turned to wilting autumn bracken. As the autumnal Sun eased its tired way towards the horizon, Dave felt his boots undesirably squelch into Sphagnum moss while all about him clumps of grass like reeds decorated the shallow boggy ground.

Approximately ten minutes later Dave carefully scrambled steeply down through a small deciduous wood of lichen speckled trees. At the wood's lower edge, he had the rarest stroke of good luck. . . it was a metalled road; not one worth writing home about you understand, if indeed you still had one. None the less it was a narrow metalled road and it beckoned and enticed him with the promise of civilisation.

"Choices, choices," he thought, "Please God let me pick the right one for a change." Dave flipped a two pound coin he'd found in his pocket, heads for left, tails for right. Heads it was but Dave glibly rejected the result for it seemed a far more inviting and easier proposition to go slightly downhill to the right.

"Silly coin," thought Dave, ignoring its solemn counsel and popping it back in his pocket, "what can a mere coin possibly know?"

And was he right!

For, indeed, only just around the next bend, set back off the road among some trees and backed by an old quarry wall, was a Pub, '*The . . .* ', well Dave couldn't make out the Pub's name as the landlord obviously wasn't over keen on either decorating or gardening. The faded sign was ardently embraced by Old English Ivy. "Could be *'The Highwayman'* with a bloke on horseback or in a Gibbet as the picture," mused Dave with a big smile, "or better still, *'The Walker's Rest'* with a picture of a big dinner, heh heh".

"It must be a popular place", he beamed to himself, as he eyed the display of posh 4x4 vehicles parked outside in the roadway.

The enticing aroma of fresh cooked food filled Dave's hungry nostrils as he approached the Pub door; a low, ledged and braced door so typical of the old cob and stone cottages of the moors, he stamped his boots a couple of times to knock off any unwelcome baggage, then squeezed the latch and opened the door. As Dave stepped inside with head lowered, the pub went quiet, it wasn't too well lit inside so he was trying to accustom his eyes when he nearly jumped out of his skin; A loud and burly voice said, "Mind yer 'ead of they beams laddie, you can get a good whack off they if y'ain't careful." Dave turned sharply to see a big solid looking man in dark, scruffy but clean clothing standing just behind the door he'd come through. "Strewth, you gave me a fright," stuttered Dave, thinking that this bloke was one sort he'd rather not meet on a dark and lonely night; great big bloke he was, had the build of a blacksmith or woodcutter. . . perhaps he was.

"I've been walking the moors a while and I'm hungry, possibly looking to find a room for the night too," Dave explained. The murmurs of conversation in the pub continued as before, as if he'd not only been accepted but was in fact a most welcomed guest.

"You've come to the right place for food," said a pretty young maid standing behind the bar, "as you can see we're very popular around these parts for our fine speciality food, you'll not find its like again on these moors. Now sir, what would sir like to drink? You'll find the menu is on the chalk board down by the inglenook. . . mind your head on the beams, you being such the fine tall fellow that you are."

Dave, being a light and casual drinker, surprised himself by ordering a pint of cider, *'local stuff'* it said in chalk on the pump label; why not, he'd give it a go. As he walked to the chalked menu board and minding his lowered head as he went, he had a chance to see what others were eating.

"Good job I'm not a vegetarian," Dave thought, as he surveyed the meat pies, stews and steaks all in vast portions. Some of the ruddy faced diners nodded to him and then to each other as though it was a ritual of some secret society. "God, these moors people are a bloody weird lot," Dave thought, "My God they are odd, still the menu looks good." In fact the menu didn't have anything written down that he hadn't already seen as he made his way among the smiling patrons at their tables. "No wonder they are smiling", Dave thought, "I haven't seen such low prices for ten years. Are they poachers? Rustlers? Who cares eh, let's eat?"

Dave returned to the bar and was gifted another smile from the girl behind the counter, "I'll have the stew please," he smiled back, "and I'll have another cider if I may. . . do you have a room for the night?"

"A good choice, the stew, sir, I'll get Chef to do you a big portion. Sit ee over there by the window sir and I'll send your drink over. I'll check on room availability sir, it won't take long," she smiled an adorable smile again. It was a long time since Dave had seen a smile like that, in fact any smile at all come to think of it. With his first cider nearly downed, yet another young lady carefully carried over his second brimful pint.

After having walked the moors with only his self to speak with, Dave was craving a little conversation and, fuelled with the effects of wild unadulterated local cider, he asked, "Have you worked here long?" Dave thought, "What a dopey question," but the girl was quite amenable to answer, "No sir, I ain't been 'ere more than a week or p'raps two. I lives with me Ma in the village, if you can call it that, about a mile that way," she pointed in the direction that the coin had earlier advised him to take. "You walking with a group sir, you know, like them rambler people sir. . . we don't often see them come round 'ere overmuch?"

Before he could answer, the young lady, of dubious social grace or intellect, was promptly called away.

"Betty, you're wanted in the kitchen. . . at once, please." Dave would only see her once again that day, then no more.

The pretty one from behind the bar, and now the sole subject of Dave's fickle and slightly inebriated affections, brought over his dinner, a huge portion of meat stew with mashed potato, "There you are sir, mind the plate, it be hot. Enjoy your meal sir, and if you don't mind we'll sort you out a room when the pub is a bit quieter. Okay my dear?" Dave nodded enthusiastically while salivating over a piece of succulent and tender meat he'd popped into his mouth. This was wonderful, just what he needed, good company, superb food, a pretty young lady who'd just elevated him from 'sir' to 'dear' and the promise of a bath and a bed for the night. At last he'd found a temporary heaven on earth.

By the time he'd finished his dinner and his fifth cider, *(yokel strength, complete with the obligatory dead rat and a horseshoe no doubt),* most if not all of the customers had left. He noticed they all did that eccentric but seemingly knowing nod, to each other, to the girl behind the bar and to the pub exit's rugged sentinel, who replied somewhat undertaker like, unsmiling and with his own sombre nod of the head.

"My God they're a weird lot out here, talk about Wicker men and hill billies, they've got nothing on this lot," mumbled Dave silently to who ever else was in his own head and still sober enough to listen."

The growingly adorable, pretty one approached Dave with a smile, "Here you are luvvy, here's a coffee and nice chocolate biscuit for you; it's on the house. Oh and here's a registration slip for you to fill in for the room. . . It'll be just the one night won't it?"

Dave smiled back a soppy smile as he was now at odds with his face muscles, having surrendered complete control of them to that firewater cider of the moors.

"Yes please you dear young thing you, by the way, I can't seem to get a mobile phone signal here, do you have a telephone I can use?" Dave had a foolish plan to phone his ex-wife and tell her how well he was doing and how he'd met new friends that cared for him . . .

"Nay, sir, you'll not get any mobile phone signal here, not in the whole valley you won't, we can't even get a TV signal you know. As for the pub phone sir, you'd be most welcome to use it for free sir. . . but the line is down and we must wait for someone to go into town and report it for us. Sorry about that, but you won't be lacking for anything after a stay here sir, you can be sure of that." The pretty one smiled her smile, gave a little curtsey then turned with a swish to return to the bar, from whence she took a keen interest in Dave's presence.

Dave looked at the registration form, lifting it towards the wall light to read each question before placing it on the table to write his answer. "Strewth, bureaucracy gone berserk even out here in the Styx", Dave mumbled under his breath, "soon they'll want next of kin too. . . . 'Blimey', they do too!" Dave thought of putting his ex-wife down, *(blissfully unaware of his Freudian slip)*, as she was the closest he'd got left in life; he thought again and simply wrote, 'Not Applicable'. "That'll do them, it's only a room for the night, not as if I'm signing away my life," he snorted a little drunken laugh.

A combination of moor weary legs and the local brew contrived to make standing more of a struggle than he'd thought it would be. Success in standing drew a little smile of achievement to Dave's face and he wandered slowly across to the bar with his registration form in hand.

"There you are my dear, shall I pay up front, and will there be a breakfast for me in the morning?" Dave inquired. Not waiting for an answer, Dave continued, "Lovely stew that, tasty meat in it, where does the pub get its supplies, local farmer?"

The pretty one was studying the registration form intently and only half heard his questions. . . "No need to pay until morning sir, breakfast is full English with local sausages, from seven thirty onwards here in the bar. . . oh, the meat supply sir is one of our Chef's greatest secrets along with his preparation methods . . . but between you and me I reckons there's a lot of cider goes along with it."

"Betty will show you to your room sir, 'Betty! Show the gentleman to his room please', have a lovely stay sir, sleep well." She smiled her lovely smile again.

Betty, roughly prodding his arm, disturbed his day dream, "This way sir. . ."

Ducking to miss even more beams and low doorways Dave followed Betty along poorly lit little corridors adorned by dusty old hunting scene paintings and the occasional chest of drawers or dresser. As they reached some rickety old stairs, lit only by a lamp in a small curtainless window at the end of the hallway, Betty stopped, she opened a dark cupboard under the stairs and said, "You can leave your walking gear in here sir if you like, it's what most other folk do."

Dave peered into the shadows to see heaps of walking gear, boots, sticks, rucksacks. . . "There's a lot of stuff in here Betty, whose is it?" Dave asked.

"Oh, it's just things that mostly them walkers must have forgot to take when they'm leaving Sir, your gear will be quite safe in there, but if you'm be afeared sir you can take it to your room, it's just that this is where the others seem to have left their stuff, that's all."

Dave, any trust he'd had in the past having all but been beaten out of him, chose to keep his gear, his life's possessions in fact, with him. Anyways, he'd secretly contrived a plan to wash some of it when he had his bath.

He had a chance, the chance to set off tomorrow with a clean slate as well as a clean T shirt, a chance for a proper new beginning.

Life encouragingly beckoned him with a smile at last.

The room was simple and comfortable enough, yet seemed furnished with things likely to have been there since the building was first occupied. It was one of three attic rooms at the back of the pub; Dave could barely see the grey quarry rock face through the small grubby rooftop window; he wiped a little grime off the glass with his sleeve; thinking out loud he mumbled he could just make out a Raven's nest, heaped with sticks on a high protected ledge. Dave wondered if the birds might roost there and in the morning he could observe them much closer than those he'd seen quartering the open moor where intelligence and years of experience had made them such a wary and elusive creature.

As Betty began to close the door and bid Dave goodnight she said, "Great big fat birds they Ravens sir, they're always hanging about around the pub. . . give me the creeps they do. You'll be seeing them again sir, you needn't have no fear of that. . . well, I'll bid 'ee goodnight sir", and the door closed behind her with the soft click of a time worn old Yale lock.

At least the pub had been modernised; although about thirty years before! However, it did have a proper bathroom and enjoying a good long soak with some of his clothes for company did him the world of good. In fact Dave drifted off quite peacefully in the warm bath, only to be woken by imagined footsteps creaking their way along the landing floorboards outside his room. Though it initially startled him he was too tired to be bothered and was in any event still under the delusional influence of the mind numbing local brew he'd supped so rashly. He settled into the old sprung bed, pulled the too short blankets up to his chest and wondered what, if anything, the morrow might bring about.

Comforted by the good food and drink, the hot bath and the fatigue of worthy effort, Dave soon fell into a deep sleep. Normally he would wake frequently and mull over the many thought provoking and oft times disturbing dreams that broke into his mind like the unwanted robbers of peace they were . . . but not this night, this night was for the sleep of the dead. . . un-waking and unknown.

The sound of a nearby Raven's call, *karronk, karronk,* brought Dave slowly out of a disorienting slumber and an almost amusing struggle to remember where he was. Slowly it all came back to him and then he dressed quickly in a clean T shirt that was now only slightly damp after a night on the bathroom towel rail. "It'll soon dry on my back," he thought as he tried to find his way back to the bar for breakfast. As Dave passed by the under-stairs cupboard he briefly shivered as if a chill had all of a sudden engulfed him, he put it down to his own silliness of wearing damp clothes to dry them off. "Dopey burke," he privately admonished himself, "When will you ever learn?"

The bar was as though he'd never left it, everything in its place, even the pretty one was there with a smile for him. "Morning to you sir, hope you slept well. Would you like tea or coffee with your breakfast? Juice and cereals are over there by your usual table", she said with summer in her voice.

"My usual table eh?" Dave thought, "It's a long time since I felt I was at home and welcome. . . lovely, this is the life for sure, I wonder why I didn't do this earlier." Dave selected a *'hair of the dog'* apple juice and sat by his window, gazing out on a bright new day, the Sun already gently warming a strip of autumn road outside.

"I might go left this time old chap," he said to another, somewhere deep inside himself.

"Yes, why not. . . let's see Betty's village that she spoke of," came an amenable reply.

When the breakfast arrived, Dave had serious doubts about being able to finish it.

"Mind the plate, it be very hot sir", said the pretty one, "we're not short on meat here and I asked the Chef to pop some extra of the special sausages on for you. Chef's compliments and he's given you four of the little beauties, now that'll set you up fine for the day sir."

Dave had other thoughts, well, more than one actually, four substantial sausages along with all the other breakfast items wouldn't set him up, it would probably set him back, and his other thought was how much he would miss that pretty smile. "You can always come back old chap, you can always come back, there's nothing to stop you now; we are free at last. . . ," again he was speaking silently to the converted, the inner self that he was only now beginning to rediscover.

Breakfast finally done and all washed, gear packed and bill paid in cash according to the pub's preferred and only method, Dave turned grudgingly towards the pub door and the beckoning outside world; he'd found a place that fulfilled his long search for happiness and he was reluctant to let it go.

"Damn it all to blazes," Dave cursed to a shocked himself as he suddenly became aware of the big silent fellow standing by the door again, then loudly to the big fellow Dave joked, "Do you stand there all night? Strewth, you make me jump; if I was older I'd be dead with a heart attack by now." Dave smiled and found himself involuntarily returning one of those weird nods that the pub seemed to like so much.

The big fellow opened the door, "Mind yer 'ead sir as ee goes, mind yer 'ead, them beams can give ee a good whack sir, you won't ever know what's 'it ee."

Rucksack in hand, Dave Baker aged forty three dreamily walked to the doorway, only hesitating to stoop and lower his head. . . the walker in him was about to begin a breathtaking new journey. . .

**

"We are the mapmakers of our own life."

**

Fremington

The Coin Collector.

No one would deny, least of all himself, that he was profoundly attached to his coin collection. Not for any monetary value you understand but for an uncanny something else he couldn't really quite explain; he'd had the collection many years, often not even remembering where a particular coin may have been unearthed. Some were the poorer remnants from childhood days when antique shops were known by their proper name. . . Junk Shops. Oh they were still full of grand and valuable items all right, violins, beautiful framed etchings, mirrors, walking sticks, stamp books of some departed ancient's collection, oil lamps and fine chairs that were once beleaguered under some plump Edwardian gentleman and there too were the coins, jam jars full of coins from around the world and from our past. A few pennies only were enough to buy these treasures, just a few new pennies for lamps of old!

One could never know or even guess where these coins had been before and what they could tell if they could but share their journey's story. Often, when a certain tranquil mood took him, he would fetch the little wooden box from the under-stairs cupboard and remove a coin to investigate further; his coins weren't protected in special folders nor were they labelled and priced. He had sold some once when he was in need of money and thereafter was to know for the rest of his life that they had in fact been priceless to his very soul. Though they were long gone to a professional collector, who had, in hindsight, ruthlessly exacted a clinical and greedy deal, he had never forgotten those coins; he still felt the pain of their loss. It was almost like they were lost children still calling to him from the grave. Sometimes he told friends of particular treasures he'd known, of Queen Ann, Napoleon, Cromwell, George and Victoria, of copper, silver and gold, of, oh so much he could recall as if only yesterday.

However, one late autumn evening, his ever welcome reunion with the coins would open his eyes and his mind to a whole new world; it could never again be just a box of coins.

He subconsciously picked out a particular coin which seemed to reach out to him as much as he to it; he put away his thoughts of yesteryear and cleaned his magnifying glass with one of those special cloths you find in spectacles cases. Soon the glass sparkled intriguingly in the electric light set above his comfortable chair in the living room.

Within minutes, the living room lights flickered forebodingly and his first thought was another bulb was on its way out; nothing lives for ever, does it? They flickered again, then darkness and silence; the fridge motor he could normally never hear, he now acknowledged by its total absence. He placed the coin in his pocket and, taking small shuffling steps in the dark, walked carefully to the kitchen where he kept a torchlight; it still worked despite the batteries having been in it for at least five years; "Perhaps some things *can* live forever", he thought, marvelling at the lamp's brightness. He checked the circuit board to find nothing had tripped out, "Must be a local area thing I guess," he mumbled to himself. Meanwhile, in the light of the torch he spotted some candles on the upper shelf, lovely bee's wax candles he'd bought for a surplus Christmas gift never yet given. "Oh, lovely, I'd forgotten all about you, you little beauties, come on, you and I can look at the coins together," he said aloud, it not escaping his attention that he sounded a bit on the eccentric side.

He cleared a place at the pine table in the kitchen, a favourite spot to sit, placed the candle in a little brass holder and lit the flame; it amused his thinking how so much could be achieved with such a tiny spark. He fetched the box and magnifying glass from the living room, returned the torch to its home in the cupboard and taking the chosen coin from his pocket sat on one of the old beech-wood chairs bathed in candle light.

The magnifying glass was old, nearly as old as he, a gift from his mother for his childhood stamp collection, yet one more thing now lost to the 'never know' land. Some of the stamps had come on letters from America, sent by long ago emigrated relatives of his; they carried a special message. . . and to this day still do. How much he would like to touch one again, an all important stamp placed with loving care to carry a message across the Ocean to family and a land they still loved and never forgot.

"Amazing how caring can lead to lasting," he thought, then remembered a pocket knife he'd been given by his grandfather; he'd not had it long before he'd lost it near his father's allotment garden. As he sat at the table lightly resting his hands, he temporarily felt the loss of that precious knife pain him. He didn't know for sure but something in him told him that the knife, an old Jack Knife, was special. It had a large blade on one side and on the other a spike for getting stones out of horse's hooves; he took a moment to imagine his Grandfather had used this knife in the Great War of 1914, or perhaps the Second World War in 1939. He would never know for sure but something drew his soul in him to think so. On reflection he realised that his soul was still connected in some way to that precious old knife; wherever it was, there was a part of him with it. Who knows, an energy or part of his grandfather's soul still had a connection with it too; Lost in time and space, yet somehow still there, something not wanting to let go.

**

He picked up the coin again, a rather interesting bronze coin with crossed rifles on the reverse, it seemed heavy to him and in fact he was finding breathing a little difficult too. "Strewth," he mumbled to himself, "I must be getting old . . . I certainly feel it tonight."

In an instant, he could smell burning, wood burning; he jumped up with a start, dropping the coin as he did, sniffing the air keenly and checking the other rooms.

"How damnable odd," he muttered half under his breath, for there was no sign of fire and nor could he any more smell burning wood; "How odd, don't say old age is giving me hallucinations now." He inwardly smiled at such possibilities, then returned to the kitchen table to continue his studies.

"Thank goodness for these lovely candles," he thought to himself, having just confirmed that it was a local area blackout by peering through the living room window . . . pitch black it was out there, not a light in sight, no Moon, no stars and no passing traffic, just pitch black, he couldn't see a thing out there, almost as if there wasn't an out there!

The candle flame welcomed him back to the kitchen with light, warmth and a strangely mystical presence, though he might deny he felt that if you were to ask him outright. *(Some things you just don't share for fear of being thought mad . . . you just keep it to yourself. . . you know what I mean, don't you?)*

He settled into his pleasurable diversion once more, picked up the coin and placed it in the palm of his left hand. Moving it closer to the light he felt a cold breeze touch him and the candle light flickered wildly, the air was thin and cold like mountain air . . . in shock he dropped the coin on the table and everything returned to normal; he felt normal, breathed easier, the candle flame was relentlessly steady and the room was warm again.

This time he knew that it would be a pointless exercise to check the windows and doors in the house . . . he knew that whatever he was experiencing was happening because of the coin, or its energy, or something. He had heard friends talk of such things, they'd told him of those who could touch an object and tell you about the owner and stuff like that, they called it psychot - something or other. He'd never really paid much attention as it all seemed highly improbable to him. . . . at that time.

On this curious and seemingly supernatural evening he decided to give it a try, what had he got to lose?

Composing his nerves and seeking the calmness he'd had at the beginning of the evening, he picked up the coin again . . . nothing! But then, as he relaxed a little more and held the coin closer to the candle light he began to see images. It was most peculiar, on the one hand he could focus on the coin and the candle and then, on the other, he could let them fade and watch what we would describe today as a video. He could see mountains, wild rugged mountains, snow clad peaks . . . he was so excited that he began to think how marvellous this was but the moment he began to think in such a way the images disappeared . He soon learned to stay relaxed and be the observer of what ever would unfold. He was on a truly amazing mind adventure.

Although the room did not overtly change again, he felt the cold mountain air and he smelled the wood smoke from a fire; it wasn't all that clear but he 'saw' a group of strangely dressed men .... They were carrying rifles, just like on the coin. He heard a name called, it sounded a bit like George but not quite, similar though. The rest of the conversation was in a strange language that he knew not but, above all, feelings welled up in him, feelings of honour and justice, hard won by armed struggle, waves of both fear and joy ebbed and flowed in him, the child in the 'seeing,' powerless; the man, victorious.

The imagery faded away but was soon replaced with different people, this time dressed in more modern clothing, it was warmer and the snow had gone but it was the same place. This time there were women also and carrying flowers which they left on the ground, and more talking too; he heard the word 'kleftis' and also what sounded like 'hero'.

It was making more sense now as he became more aware of the context; he was witnessing a family returning to mark a significant monument in their distant family history, about a man who lived long ago, first as a robber then as a national hero. The people standing there now, talking, singing and leaving the flowers were descendants of this man, the hero, George or Georgius. Feelings of compassion, empathy, connection and pride coursed powerfully through his very being. This commemorative Greek coin must have been there with them that day on that mountain, carried in one of their pockets; the coin's aura had first absorbed and now it was to impart this experience to a receptive mind, his mind.

The lights in the house flickered once then burned steadily, mains power 'restored'. The spell was broken for the evening and he gazed thoughtfully at the coin in his hand wondering why he should feel such affinity with such an insignificant and moderately recent Greek coin. He placed it back in the little wooden box and went to put the kettle on.

Glancing at the clock he realised that the power must have been off for about thirty minutes or so, with his cup in hand he returned to the table and blew out the candle. For the life of him he just couldn't remember what had happened in that lost time, not a bit of it.

"Must have slipped off into a day dream . . . it's true, you're just getting old, come on old chap, time for bed," he said aloud, it not escaping his attention that he sounded a bit on the eccentric side.

**

"Change the way you look at things, and the things you look at will change".

**

Fremington Quay

The Young Mariner's Return.

It all began, not that many years ago, with the Richmond family's holiday disaster. (That being Mrs Richmond's final and considered opinion on the matter). Life would never be the same again, not after that holiday!

"Cycling and camping, you just can't beat it," beamed a contented Dave Richmond to himself as he dragged his reluctant family along the Tarka trail from Barnstaple. He paused for a while to catch his breath and sensed the promise of a cool September evening mist drawing ever closer. Closer too came his distraught wife and highly agitated children, as they pedalled hard to catch him up.

"Why on earth couldn't we have taken a B&B in town?" pleaded his wife Caroline, gasping for breath. The two, temporarily mum supportive girls, Lucy 12 and Lizbeth 9 enthusiastically agreed.

Dave ignored their reluctance to continue, "Are we men or mice, eh? When I was in the boy scouts we did this all the time. You'll love it! Trust me. Just up ahead is a quaint and historic place called Fremington Quay, I'll treat you all to a warm meal at the café. . . come on . . . last one there's a big sissy." With that he was gone, pedalling as fast as he could go.

There were however a number of relevant considerations that Dave hadn't fully grasped. One. The girls weren't, nor ever would be, boy scouts. Two. The café was not only closed but was also temporarily deserted. Three. Time had given him a rose tinted and favourably distorted view of the dubious pleasures of autumnal camping.

As Dave approached the deserted Quay, his heart sank; he could plainly see it was closed and with not a living soul in sight. What would his family say? He resolved to put on a brave face and pretend it was all part of his plan, the great adventure. "The rich tapestry of life itself," he'd tell them. "We'll camp here tonight," he said pointing to a flat grassed area close by the now full River Taw; it wasn't so far off high water slack and the nearby long drowned mud banks lay patiently waiting for the ebb tide so they would see light and breathe air once again.

There were lots of moans and groans but they had little choice, for both night and river mist had arrived and they didn't know where else they could go. Dave did of course. . . But 'defeat' wasn't an option. As leader of the family he had a face to save. . . his own!

This was one decision that would prove to haunt the family for longer than they could possibly imagine.

Their two tents were soon pitched and the little camping gas burner warmed their hands as well as some reserve soup rations. The family didn't stay long outside. Despite it being early, the penetrating dark cold of the river mist forced them to retreat to the sleeping bag warmth of their tents.

"Not too long with those little lamps, girls! Those batteries must last you all week. We didn't have such luxuries in the boy scouts you know. . . Night, night, sleep well," advised Dave, his voice somewhat muffled by his own sleeping bag. The girls just about heard their mother asking if he'd also worn that silly woolly hat to bed in the boy scouts. They giggled a little at the thought and then lay there chatting very quietly with their lamps on, obscured from parental eyes by their sleeping bags. Eventually Lizbeth fell asleep but Lucy was lying on lumpy ground that felt more like stones than grass; move as she might it was difficult to be comfortable. Insomnia and the cold kept her fitfully awake for a couple of hours listening to the sound of her sister's breathing, the occasional snore from the neighbouring tent and the silence, the otherwise total silence. It was the silence she could hear more than anything.

Then she heard it. . . a far off creaking noise from the direction of the river. Now she was eyes staring wide awake, she fumbled for her little torch. Oh no! She'd left it switched on by mistake and now its life hung on by the faintest orange glimmer. She could hear splashing in the river nearby, accompanied by a sort of knocking noise; she stopped breathing to hear it the better. Then there was silence again. By now she was too frightened to make a single sound; Lucy began to sense a presence beyond the tent, an invisible presence that was able to pass through the tent fabric and then, the strangest of feelings. It was most peculiar, like putting her feet in a lukewarm bath but from the inside. The unstoppable feeling slowly completed its journey to the top of her head. Nothing bad was happening, she felt fine, it was just an odd feeling that she soon seemed to get used to, after about an hour of wakefulness and puzzlement Lucy drifted off, at times she even felt like she was being rocked gently to sleep.

Morning came with the sound of agitated dog walkers calling their dogs away from scent marking the family tents. Dave was first up, complete with woolly hat and a determination to lead the way again. He put the kettle on the burner and went across the heavily dewed grass to investigate the boarded up and now obviously deserted cafe in daylight. By the time he returned, Caroline had already made some hot drinks and was chatting to a shivering Lizbeth. "And where's Lucy then?" he asked, "We didn't get to lie in when we were in the boy scouts you know."

He was cut short by a stern, uncompromising look from his wife, "She's not feeling too well, had an awful night's sleep, bad dreams and all that, just not herself today. . . I told you we should have gone B&B, why not listen for once?" scolded Caroline, thinking it was a pity that the boy scouts hadn't bestowed her husband with the benefit of a bit more common sense.

Their holiday was cut short and they went home and back to normal, everyone that is, except Lucy. Lucy didn't eat too well, lost concentration easily and spent most of her time talking about the strange dreams she was having, dreams of being places she had never heard of never mind visited; dreams where she felt pain, cold and loneliness; dreams came that left Lucy gasping for breath and in a state of blind panic calling for her mother in the dark.

Of course Caroline took her to the doctors but they didn't have any idea what to do, if anything they were all at sea, not knowing what to do, their advice was just the usual stuff that might with luck fit something they didn't understand. Then one day the family doctor suggested seeing a psychiatrist. . . "Stone the crows," Dave whispered to his wife, "do they think she's gone mad? Why see this psycho whatever person? She'll be fine, just needs a bit more time that's all." But time wasn't going to change anything, Lucy continued to have the dreams and the dreams continued to be the unhappy same.

A month later they were visiting the outpatients department at the nearest Psychiatric Unit and seeing a really kind young lady who spent an hour or so chatting to Lucy. As Lucy and her dad walked to the car chatting about the 'nice lady', Caroline was being given a findings report and most likely conjecture on Lucy's problem. "Well she's a lovely little girl, seems quite normal to me, I think we can put it down to an over-active imagination coupled with the trauma of camping out in the cold and damp against her wishes. I suspect it is a subconscious rebellion thing. I'm sure she'll be fine, just give it a bit more time. . . perhaps take her out in the sunshine to a park or boating lake or something similar; So glad to have been of help; always feel free to call on us again, bye, bye Mrs Richmond."

Caroline was not the least bit impressed with the system's tardy and so called 'help' but did however take the girls out to the park for a picnic in the sunshine. While they were all enjoying the little treats Caroline had provided, Lucy suddenly went white and almost stopped breathing. . . "What's wrong?" panicked Caroline, "what is the matter Lucy?"

Taking a gasp of breath, "That noise, mum, that's the noise, the one I heard at the Quay that night, that clonk, clonk noise. . . just like that it was, then it went quiet," exclaimed Lucy.

"Oh, Lucy, look, it's just someone in a rowing boat, it's the noise the oars make against the boat, see, look, 'splash, clonk, clonk', it's just a rowing boat that's all," assured her mother. Sadly by then the mood had changed for the worse and the family returned home. Caroline was at her wits end to help her daughter and was telephoning a good friend about her woes when her friend made a strange suggestion, "I know a medium," she said, a really good one, no mumbo jumbo stuff, really good. I can ask for you if you like."

"I'll check with Dave first, I doubt he'll go for something like that, he's always ridiculed such things in the past; I'll check with him and get back to you, thank you though for your kindly support," Caroline said, thoughtfully replacing the receiver slowly.

As it happened and to Caroline's great surprise Dave was all for it, "we must help the poor girl, even if it is mumbo jumbo as long as it works then, who cares? All we want is to have our daughter back, back home with us from wherever her mind has gone. Phone them back, we'll give it a try."

She gave him a hug, "thank you, thank you, I'll phone her back right away."

**

The evening of the 'medium' arrived, as did the medium herself, a dear little old lady called Hilda. Hilda had lots of grandchildren of her own and was soon at one with the girls, they seemed to warm to her immediately.

"Going well so far," whispered Dave to his wife. "Shhshh dear, let's not speak unless asked," she replied.

Hilda and Lucy sat close together on the bottom two steps of the stairwell while the rest of the family sat on the carpeted hallway floor, leaned against the walls and listened intently.

In a soft comforting voice, Hilda began, "Well, Lucy, I hear you have been having some strange dreams that don't really fit your own experiences in life. I'll tell you a secret, just between me and you; that's because sometimes they are not just our own dreams but sometimes belong to someone else. I think I can tell you about the 'someone else' in your case and how we can get them to stop. It is a boy, not much older than you and he is a lost soul, he needs our help to go home, we can help him quite easily. What do you say? Shall we have a go?"

Lucy nodded with a smile; she felt empowered by Hilda's presence and was beginning to feel more in control of her fears. Intuitively, Hilda picked up on Lucy's unspoken feeling and agreed, "Yes Lucy, a fear, once it's understood, no longer frightens us, strange isn't it?" "Okay, dear, I'll tell you what I know and you just stop me at any time to add something or ask a question, alright, my lovely? We are going back in time, to the birth of this boy to a poor family, it is 1836, at a place, you probably never heard of, Fremington Quay . . . ".

Lucy interrupted excitedly, "I know it, I know it, that's where we went on holiday and the dreams started. . ." Hilda smiled; she now knew for sure she was on the right track.

"I see a young boy growing up," Hilda continued, "a name is coming to me. . . Leonard, Leonard. . . "

"Goulde," said Lucy excitedly interrupting, "I don't know how I know, it just came into my mind, just now."

"Yes," said Hilda, "you are right, Leonard Goulde he is indeed. When he was only about twelve years of age, reluctantly he had to be sent to sea by his father who could no longer afford to feed him. I sense the sobbing heartache of his mother. A couple of years later his ship returned to the Quay and without seeking permission Leonard took the ship's small boat and rowed ashore in the mist to find his family. They were not there; no where to be seen, he looked and looked but could not find them. He looked so long that by then the mist hidden ebb flow was at its peak; his strength and little boat were no match for the current as he desperately tried to find and reach his ship. Well the sad thing is, with the ebbing current so powerful, he drowned, we can't change that, that's what happened. Now that might explain why you have held your breath at times when his presence was close. Anyway, ever since then on certain September nights when the mist and the tide are as on his final and fateful night, Leonard returned, still searching for his beloved family. Unless we help him he will search forever," Hilda paused, "are you still okay with this Lucy?"

Lucy nodded enthusiastically, this was the first time anybody had understood what she was experiencing and she felt completely safe with Hilda.

"I think," confided Hilda to Lucy, "that the cold, the fear and your need for home that night, coincided with the very feelings Leonard experienced and that 'fear' connected the dead with the living. . . through a sort of gateway.

We can re-open that gate and set him free too. I have an idea."

Looking up at Caroline, who was watching spellbound by the revelations, Hilda suggested, "Tomorrow, after school, let the three of us go to the records office in Barnstaple town and see if we can find our Leonard. We might also find our answer there."

"Yes," added Lucy, "poor Leonard will never find his family with me, he needs to go back home to find them."

**

The next day they met at the records office and kindly staff brought them the records they needed. "Try the 1841 Census first," they'd suggested.

Looking through the pages, Hilda found a Goulde, Leonard, "Here he is, it says age five," she said pointing, "And, here, look, his father, a William Goulde, coal porter."

Lucy reached out and placed her finger on the name below, "Mother," she said in a soft voice that intimated a long awaited reunion. Poignancy not lost on Hilda but who knew when to say nothing.

"Next try the 1851 census", advised the archivists, and produced the Fremington Quay documents. They all looked, but nothing to be seen, no Goulde family recorded as living there in 1851. They searched in vain, as too had Leonard on that desperate night. "Oh, that poor boy," sighed Hilda, It looks like when he returned from sea they weren't there; poor child, so young to be away from his family, life was simply harder for everyone then for sure."

"They could have moved any time after 1841," staff suggested, "You could look for baptisms for other children but that would take some time, let's look in the index for Goulde in other parishes for the 1851 census."

There were a couple of possible references but one in particular looked promising, "there he is," said a staff member, "look, here, William Goulde, still working as a coal porter and living in Pilton down by the Yeo Quayside , and it looks like the family have three more children at this time too."

Lucy peered closer at the page, "Yes, oh yes!" Lucy proclaimed, "This is my family," not realising what she was saying, but Hilda knew and hid a smile, "This is them."

As they walked to the car park, Hilda gave Lucy a hug around the shoulders, "you don't need me any more dear, what you need to do is return with your family to Fremington Quay one misty evening when the tide is as it was the night you camped and the gateway will be open for Leonard to go home again. Now we have shown him where to find his mother he can make his own way. You can feel proud of yourself; you have saved a desperate and lonely soul from a never ending search which trapped him in another place and time. I am so proud of you, well done. Now I must also say goodbye, we will not forget each other, will we?"

Lucy gave her a big hug and thanked Hilda for saving 'her own soul', as she put it. Hilda got into the little car that was waiting for her with her husband, Fred, and with a final wave, was gone.

**

It had been a year of mystifying hell but all seemed worthwhile now they understood. The family drove one misty afternoon to the Quay cafe to follow Hilda's instructions. The cafe was quiet, only the owners present; The Richmond's enjoyed hot drinks and home made cake and were made most welcome. The family shared their secret and their troubles into the early evening, the young owner and his wife kept open as if they had invited friends and family in their company.

After a couple of hours Lucy rose calmly and said, "I'm just going for a little walk, I won't be going far."

Dave wanted to go with her or at least wanted to tell her to keep away from the edge but something inside him told him to be quiet and that all would be well. There is a time to trust.

Lucy, now almost spirit like herself, walked slowly in the sea mist, across the heavily dewed grass towards the river. As she came to the railings she stopped and whispered, "Goodbye Leonard, safe journey, say hello to your mum for me. I'm sure she waited everyday for you to come home. God bless, bye, bye." Lucy sensed that she was now standing all alone; alone with a tear in her eye, a tear of happiness for Leonard whose soul she had touched and he hers. Only Lucy's ears that night would hear the splash of water and the clonk, clonk of ghostly oars in rowlocks. Invisible in the September mist, a little boat was eagerly being rowed up river on a flowing tide towards Pilton and the peace of coming home at last.

Lucy stood a moment or two, surrounded by a peace of her own, then returned to the café.

"Time to go home now mum, just the four of us this time," exclaimed a beaming Lucy standing in the doorway.

Life could never be the same again. . . it could only be better.

**

"Night has brought to those who sleep only dreams they cannot keep. "
Enya.

"Wisdom and compassion are ever the best of companions."

**

Glenthorne area

Pathway into the Darkling.

High up on a hill that bordered the moor, a tall aging man sat thoughtfully in the old Inn, a mid day log fire warmed his heart as well as his body; he slid his empty plate away  across the wooden table, reclined on the high backed bench seat and enjoyed the last of his red wine. Outside, glorious late winter sunshine beckoned both his soul and boots to join in its travels and to walk a while in its company.

Some few years ago before this day, he had walked along the nearby coastal path and had become lost, the path seemingly having just vanished, an unfortunate habit exhibited by most of the paths he followed, in the end he'd found his way via streams, mud, thorn and fence back to the main road. He never could understand where the path had gone; even a later and thorough scrutiny of a detailed map gave him no clues. It occurred to him that should he walk from the opposite direction it might prove easier to follow the path and the puzzle would at long last be solved. Today then was the day to put his plan and himself to the test.

A handshake and cheery farewell to the landlord and moments later he left the comfort and safety of the Inn and walked across the road to the car park, pulling on his woolly hat against the winter chilled wind as he went. He had a plan; he knew of some coastal path signposts a few miles east and set off in search. The deserted and undulating tarmac road across the moors was pleasantly decorated with the occasional cattle grid and agreeable far reaching wilderness views. He parked his car on a desolate earth lay-by, checked the contents of the car seemed safe and set off on foot to find the valley that would lead to the sea.

His mind was taken by a sign that read, 'Site of ancient Barrow.' It wasn't in his direction but, what the heck, it could only be a small detour, so he walked in the direction indicated by the lichen covered finger post. It took a little longer than he'd anticipated but he eventually found and marvelled at the site, imagining what it would have been like in the days when it was built; he stood on a high point and enjoyed the commanding view of the valleys around, just as they who built it there must have done. He sensed that his feelings were also their feelings and as such he was welcome there in that ancient place.

His plan was changing all the time now but he was enjoying it all so much, the view, the air, and the sunshine . . . the raw, hallowed connection with nature itself. He decided to walk further afield and in the downhill direction of the beach some one mile distant. At first his way was barred by thick undergrowth and fences but he eventually found a track that took him what could be the right way.

How pleased he was he'd made the effort, for the beach was surreally beautiful and obviously rarely visited; he stayed a while looking at patterns in the stones and the amusing antics of a friendly Robin. Perhaps he'd stayed too long but it was such a wonderful day and he was sure he could easily retrace his steps.

It was a relentless but steady 1,000 feet climb back up to the road where he had earlier abandoned his car but first he had to climb over the land slipped fallen tree that blocked the path and had so nearly kept him from reaching the beach. It was a climb for a younger man than he but the day was good and there seemed a touch of youth in his being . . . in his old mind there was anyway.

So far so good, he'd kept to a track he'd found which he believed would meet up with the one he'd used for the descent; he felt he'd reached about a third of the way up from the beach. However, a quick look at his watch and a glance at the lowering Sun told him he'd better get on with it, no more dilly dallying, time for serious walking.

He stopped for a moment to catch his breath and looked back to see how far he'd come when he realised, horror of horrors, that he was on the wrong track, he was climbing on the wrong side of the wooded valley. . . he needed to be the other side, on the other hill, damn it all.

You'd think that a chap who'd become lost so many times before would have thought differently. . . but he didn't. With a misplaced confidence far exceeding his questionable ability, he decided to cut across country through the woods, taking a straight line for where he thought he'd find his car; it was to turn out to be one of his more regrettable decisions.

He stepped off the track and at first the open deciduous woodland was reasonably easy going, despite the trauma of finding a meatless dismembered sheep carcass on the way. As he drove his body onward, his mind dwelled morbidly about the dead sheep, how it might have met its end and old wives tales of big cats out on the moors. The hairs stood up on the back of his neck and his body gave an involuntary shudder.

The easy going underfoot stopped abruptly at a barbed wire fence, beyond which the climb was thick with old conifers. He walked along the stout wire fence looking for an easier way through. 'Mmm,' he thought, 'they built this to keep you out and no doubt about that, why on earth would they want such a fence here?' With an unusual touch of luck he found an easier bit; there were some signs that someone had been through there before, probably with their dog, as a few strands of black fur were still hooked on the wire.

'Damn it, damn it, damn the wire,' he cursed as the sharp metal barbs hooked on his clothing and he suffered a small but annoying cut trying to extricate himself. 'Oh well, not too bad old boy,' he said trying to console himself and pressing his coat sleeve on the back of his bleeding hand, 'it'll soon stop, you'll be fine,' he muttered and, lowering his head to go under the dead branches of a large conifer, he walked on, upwards and onwards. A lost man will never understand what drives him forward into an unknown that defies logic and sensibility and he was no exception to that madness.

There was a darkness about the forest, a darkness in more ways than one; he was not comfortable with his route, often having to change direction to avoid tangles of dead but impenetrable lower branches. In the end it was only the hill itself that told him he was going in the right direction; sort of right direction anyway. Trees and ground became a little lighter up ahead and he hoped he was at the end; it turned out to be a small clearing where living trees had once stood but had been felled by nature's course and following the great leveller's plan that all will pass that way.

At least it gave him a breather from walking stooped with head down through the forest. As he crossed the clearing, on the remnant of a lone standing tree, he noticed what looked like raking scratch marks; vertical, they were wide, deep and reached nearly as high as he was tall. Thoughts of a big cat immediately overwhelmed his mind and he looked around intently, staring into the encroaching forest gloom; he looked for something to use as a weapon. . . a small stone came to hand but his mind mocked him, 'not big enough for the neighbourhood cat,' he threw it down and picked up a branch the length of a broom handle. He tested it against the unknown beast's scratching post; his erstwhile 'protector' swiftly snapped in two. All the pieces of wood that littered the clearing were the same, after all, that's why they were down there. . . they were there on the forest floor because they were weak – and dead!.

He knew that he must move on quickly, for time was against him and he was soon going to have to move from this bright clearing into the unknown dark of that blasted forest. . . oh, how he wished he'd gone another way. As he moved uphill to the first conifers his mind foolishly and almost unwillingly reminded him of films he'd seen on television about Leopards and Mountain Lions dropping on to their prey from above and with ferociously inescapable jaws gripping the throat to end all breath, all life. . . clever, silent, powerful killers. These thoughts stopped him in his tracks for a moment while he frightened himself even more by images of big cats following the scent of blood. . . his blood.

Terror drove his legs without thought into the darkening forest, he dared not look up for fear of what he might see, he watched the ground intently where he placed his boots, not wishing to slip or to look weak enough to become another hidden meal in the forest.

Nobody, had ever walked through there, he realised that now and the black fur he'd seen wasn't left by any black Labrador either. There was no one for miles, no one would hear him scream; the days when fields were full of farm labourers fixing walls and cutting hedges by hand were long gone, they went long before the big cats turned up, set loose by the thoughtless and self interested rich. . . 'Damn them, damn them all,' he thought as sweat began to soak his once warm dry clothes. He walked desperately, he breathed hard and he felt alone; afraid, tearful and alone.

He must have stumbled on for another twenty minutes or so, the trees seemingly trying to trap him with their low branches or trip him with the fallen. Easier looking pathways sprang up to lure him deeper into the unknown. . . his keen ears listened for any noise, no birds had he heard, no sign of life, everything was expectantly silent. . . it seemed everything, even the trees, were listening, watching, holding their breath, for a beginning as well as an ending to the unfolding drama.

Suddenly there was a commotion somewhere behind him, a great crashing noise of something running through the trees impervious to the dead branches that reached out to stop it. Whatever it was, was coming his way, for a moment he was frozen in time and space, frozen by fear as his mind raced to decide on fight or flight. An adult deer, don't ask what sort, but it was a deer, bounded and crashed itself past him only a few metres away, it didn't see him, it had eyes only for escape. The sound of the deer disappeared into the distance and all was quiet again, his legs shook with fright itself, adrenalin flooded his body, he stared intently in the direction from whence the deer had bolted. . . nothing, only silence and darkness, both of which appeared to him to be ever sneaking stealthily closer.

He turned up his coat collar and donned his old fawn woolly gloves as if to protect himself. . . they wouldn't of course but strangely it did make him feel safer. Well, life or death; it was the least he could do to invoke all that remained of his power to extricate himself from this catastrophic mess of his own making. . . he walked with renewed determination up that confounded hill; like the fleeing deer, not noticing anything but the way ahead, not thinking of anything but the danger behind.

It was an increasingly dark struggle as time drew on to evening but by then his night vision was improving and he could still just make out the way ahead, then a chill breeze hit his face and bright stars took the place of trees. . . he'd made it. . . just the fence to cross and he was free of the forest shroud at last. Beyond a hedge, a speeding car's headlights showed where the road passed by, only an open field away from where he stood. Pain and fear seemed to evaporate as he strode purposefully away from the forest, although he couldn't resist pausing and taking a long final look back into the abyss of darkness behind him. To this day he'll tell you he is not sure if in that darkness he saw the feint glimmer of two steady green eyes, watching, watching him get away. Then they too were gone, as if they never were. He never looked for that lost path again.

**

"They who only walk on sunny days will never complete their journey."
Vietnamese proverb.

**

Great Torrington

Children of the Gingerbread house.

(Another family 'ghost' story filled with puns about knitting. Based on real events and people).

The time to leave was looming ever closer for Dave, who had hoped for a very different Saturday indeed. "Right, come on kids, get a move on, toys in the box, we're off to some old knitting exhibition your mum wants to see," said father of two Dave, as he jingled his car keys impatiently in his hand. Dave shouted up the stairs for his wife Becky, "Come on dear, we're all ready to go. . . your mum's here too." Dave raised his eyes slightly to the heavens, why his wife was never ready or why she'd invited her mum to this 'knitting thing', he'd never understand. "What is it with knitting anyway?" He thought deeply to himself.

Becky's voice from outside the open front doorway suddenly brought him back from his pensive state, "Come on then you woolly headed nit wit, let's be having you, you're always last," she said in a happy, joking manner.

Not long after, they were all neatly strapped into their seats in the family car and safely on their way with Dave at the wheel,

Becky beside him with the exhibition brochure and squeezed between the two child seats at the back, his mother-in-law, Mavis.

Katie was four and a half and Luke, three and a half. . . both had wild imaginations; Too wild sometimes for Dave, who was more down to earth about most things – okay, everything.

On arrival at the exhibition hall, by sheer luck they found one parking space left. With the children already made increasingly hyper by their grandmother's tales and over liberal sweetie hand outs, Dave said, "Okay, Becky, I'll wait here I think, how long will you be?"

Becky gave him an icily derisory look that made it quite clear that he was joining them inside and would be enjoying it, regardless.

They were all welcomed into the hall by a nice lady called Alison who told the children they too could knit something if they wished but the children only had eyes for a little house made of wool. Alison felt their excitement at seeing the gingerbread house and called a volunteer over to show them around.

"You can call me Sean," he said with a big friendly smile as he led them closer to the best 'doll's house' Katie had ever seen. Even

Dave was impressed- and not much in life ever did that.

The adults marvelled at the knitting prowess and constructive imagination of the builders of the Gingerbread house and Sean explained some of the features in depth, "It is also filled with wonders from the world of wool and knitters," he said, "the original didn't have a fence but we added that and the gate to keep the public out ... people tried to rearrange the furniture to their own liking, children were put to bed in there so the parents could wander off for some peace, we had to vacuum picnic crumbs out of it and once found a homeless chap had moved in." "Anyway," said Sean, who could obviously spin a good yarn, "just touch some of the items in the garden; have an open mind and just reach over the fence ... touch a flower." As they obliged him by doing so, he continued, "there, can you feel it? Can you sense the sort of person who knitted that piece, ask yourself; was it an old lady or a child?"

Dave admitted he could feel nothing, Becky thought perhaps she could but was a bit reluctant to commit to an answer for fear of being wrong. However, Mavis was well into this 'game' and flitted from item to item proclaiming with utter confidence who might have knitted what and even where.

Suddenly Becky issued a shrieking and blunt command to the children, "Stop! You two, you stop right there, now come on out of the garden."

By now, Katie and Luke were up to the front door of the Gingerbread house. "It's okay lady, don't worry, they're safe there," assured Sean. Becky wasn't thinking of their safety, she was thinking of how much damage they might do to the contents of this beautifully presented monument to the skills of countless knitters across the world.

Sean reassured Becky once again, "Look, we don't normally do this, but you're lovely people and I can see the children want to see what treasures there may be inside. I'm only a stand-in guide while Colin is away looking at croft retreats in Shetland and knitting holidays in San Marino. It's very quiet at the moment and if you promise not to make it known to others, I'll take you inside." Sean's offer was met with three solemn nods in hushed and secret silence. Somehow Dave had found himself joining in, involuntarily. "Weird that," he thought.

They ducked their heads to enter in through the low door as the children pushed with strong hands past their legs to be in first. It was lighter inside than they thought it would be and immediately felt comfortably homely. As Becky and her mum gazed in wonder on row upon row of intricately knitted objects on knitted shelves, Dave was looking in horror, as though someone had sat on it, at a big dent in the otherwise beautifully made up bed, "What have you done to the bed kids? You're not to climb on things, for Pete's sake do not touch stuff."

"It wasn't us," protested a very defensive Katie, "it's a nice old lady knitting, and she's got a pet sheep called Barbara."

At this point Dave gave up, the children were living in a different world to him and he certainly wasn't going to encourage them by continuing the conversation, "Well don't touch things again, okay?"

Katie and Luke weren't even listening by now as they stroked Barbara's lovely clean fleece. Barbara even told them of her famous grandfather who had come from Ireland where the leprechauns live, his name was Lan O'Lin from County Scane and surely they must have had heard of him, why hundreds would flock to see him at the grand summer farm fairs. Barbara was obviously very proud of her lineage.

"We can knit Dave a cardigan, mum, couldn't we?" said Becky.

"We certainly could and it would be far nicer than some of those cast off things he gets from the charity shop, there are some nice colours in here to choose from. Look Dave, what about this pink one," smiled a cheekily knowing Mavis.

"You must be joking, I wouldn't be seen dead in that," Dave retorted.

"You're wasting your time mum, you're casting pearls before swine with that one," Becky said, joining her mum with the joke.

"Sean," said Mavis, "should the house have been knitted with climbing plants on it?"

"What makes you ask that?" replied Sean, puzzled by the question.

"Well, you may think me strange but I keep hearing the word 'Ivy' in my head, and I just wondered, that's all," said Mavis, wishing she'd not said anything now.

"No, I'm not surprised because when I enter the gingerbread house I too hear things in my mind, I think it's like some energy left in the knitting, you know, the thoughts and feelings of the people who handled the wool and stuff. I'll ask Alison about Ivy later and see what she says," assured Sean thoughtfully.

Dave's eyes rolled skywards again, he couldn't feel any 'energies' in the room except it was getting a little warm and his two children were all the energy he could cope with today anyway.

Katie and Luke ran about shrieking and laughing, they said they were chasing sheep. Dave turned to Becky, "we need a sheep dog ourselves to keep control of these two, I think it's time we went home before they wreck the joint."

"Mum, mum, can we take something with us, go on, please mum, go on mum." . Katie and Luke chanted in that clever way that only children know.

Thinking what a clever move he'd made and that he'd out foxed them this time for sure, Dave told them, "All right, all right, if you must, you can bring the little old knitting lady off the bed and her pet sheep Bobby if you must . . . ".

"Barbara, Dad, Barbara," they shouted in unison.

After some brief but fond goodbyes to Sean and Alison, their little car crunched across the gravel of the now empty car park and turned right for the road home.

"What a good day after all," thought Dave. Becky was going to cook them all a special meal for teatime and he was going to be able to watch his favourite football match on the as yet unseen highlights programme; the day was fine and the family car was running beautifully too, all except for an intermittent click clack noise, which Dave put down to a couple of stones in the tyres, probably picked up in the exhibition car park. Clutching her handbag on her lap, his mother-in-law was fast asleep between two excitedly chattering children. "God only knows who they think they're talking to", thought Dave, "what wild imaginations they have for sure."

**

"Our day is but a path we tread, a gentle path among possibilities."
Kent Nerburn

**

Loxhore and Challacombe area.

Life, on the moors

As in a life, so to, a story can have a variety of endings, each of them created by choices made in the mind of the reader. In this story you will

inevitably come across choices with which you may or may not agree. Such is the way of life.

This is the thought provoking tale of a late 18th Century peasant family as they struggle across desolate moor-land seeking a better life on the other side, a place free from betrayal and starvation. Will they find it? Will they make the right choices? More importantly, would you?

The date is 1786 and like many peasants of the day, George Dinnicombe was another hard working victim of the social system, often surviving on subsistence wages in return for giving his all, his life, his family and his soul. He was hungry, not just for decent food but for the opportunity to provide well for his family. George himself was born to pauper parents in the winter of 1752 and when old enough to work was given away and bound to a Thomas Reid, owner of a blacksmiths and farriery business not far from the pretty Devon village of Loxhore.

George did well as apprentice to Thomas Reid, a kindly and likeable gentleman with an excellent reputation for horses and ironwork. George proved himself over again as a willing worker and a keen learner and soon became indispensable to the Reid's family business. Life was as good as could be expected for a working class man.

Earlier, in 1774, then age twenty two, George had married Phoebe. Phoebe Goulde was a God fearing and kind-hearted young lass from Stoke Rivers, she also came from an impoverished family, her father having succumbed to Smallpox the year before she was twenty and married. The couple was blessed with three children, all healthy and strong - William 11, Thomas 9, and their sister Sarah 6.

Old Mr Reid, the owner of the business had two grown sons, Mark and his younger rival sibling Luke, of whom it must be said was a downright wastrel and a most disappointing son for the fair minded and kindly Thomas Reid. It was a bad day for all when Thomas Reid was finally laid to rest. Thomas' funeral was a fine affair and well attended by the local community, in particular the many that were in his debt for past favours. None were surprised by the absence of the spendthrift Luke, who had ridden into Barnstaple town to celebrate his inheritance in the only way he knew. Subsequently his drinking and gambling incurred debts upon the business and despite his brother Mark's best efforts they soon had to let workers go and evicted loyal and trusty servants of many years.

On the third of March 1786 it was George's turn and he was the last to go. The business had failed completely by then, due to Luke's so called 'friends' calling in their markers.

Mark Reid retained a small cottage from the estate in which he continued to live with his grieving mother. None of their employees could be afforded such luxuries. None of these events were going to be easy for anyone. By the dying heat of the forge, the two men stood in solemnity already aware of the other's mind, 'I'm deeply sorry George. We've grown up together here and I had great hopes we would all grow old in dignity and peace together too. It's not to be. The cottage you live in is no longer mine. You will have to move out, I'm truly sorry. I can tell you how bad it is, the horses we have, those few that are left, I cannot even afford to feed. I'm not sure how I will survive but am hopeful one of my father's friends may have pity on me and find me a position.'

'I'm sorry too sir for your loss, don't you worry about us sir, I shall think of something. . . don't you worry sir. I shall go and speak with Phoebe and we'll make our plans,' said George with a confidence in his voice that belied his sense of total loss. Mark had been like a brother to him all these years and old Mr Reid had been like a kindly uncle all through his service. It wasn't the first time George had struggled alone and he didn't suppose it would be the last either. As he walked away from the smithy, across the once weed free, inner cobbled yard and under the barn to the lane outside, he met Luke coming the other way. As usual he was the worse for drink but treated George with the respect that bullies often have for those who are in nature and in stature their betters, 'Sorry to see you go George old chap, you're a fine fellow, fine wife too I'll say.'

Something in the back of his mind inspired George to ask a favour, 'Luke, sir, if you cannot feed the horses, could you see your way to let me have one in payment for all the times I saved you from troubles in the past?'

'George old chap, help yourself, no, tell you what, I'll pick one out myself and tether her outside the barn for you. That big bay with the black mane is a fine horse. You leave it with me. You can trust me not to let you down.' With that he staggered off to confront his poor brother over some trifling amount he still needed.

George walked thoughtfully to the comparative hovel they called a cottage but nevertheless a home of happy times, an emerging plan taking shape in his mind. At the back of the cottage was a run down open farm cart in need of some attention, what with that fine horse Luke had promised and a few running repairs to the cart they could use it to start a new life where there was more work. Many a traveller seeking the farrier at the smithy had shared their tales of riches and fine living in towns such as Bristol. Riches fostered by the ships that sailed to and from the new world. This was a bold but fine plan.

Phoebe listened quietly as he broke the news. She thought a while then said quietly, 'Why George dear, could they not tell you last week when you would have had a chance of work at the hiring fair. You are a good man with fine skills, you would have found work to be sure. . . and now it is three months to the next one. . . and us homeless with winter not yet past.' 'That Luke will surely go to hell, for certain he should, I pity his poor mother, God bless her.' The children, though not fully understanding the implications, had heard the news. They had such faith in their father, they were not afraid, it seemed like an adventure.

'We will leave tomorrow morning. While I prepare the cart you must gather what little we have to take. There may be a few root vegetables still good enough to lift. . . William, you can do that. Otherwise just help your mother in whatever she asks. While there is some daylight left I will begin on the old cart,' and with that he was gone to the rear of the cottage, tools in hand.

That night they all had a good supper and kept the fire banked well, no point in leaving firewood for the next tenant. Nobody slept well that night, all minds in turmoil over the unknown.

As a pale grey March dawn approached slowly from the east bringing with it a cold wind off the moors, George was already preparing to leave. He had on his working clothes and thick coat as his old boots clumped up the stony lane for one last time to the stables. He was in for a dreadful shock, no fine bay horse awaited him, just an old nag of twenty years or more. The poor animal was more suited to feeding the hounds at his Lordship's hunt than pull a cart.

George was staring at the old grey mare in a mixture of disbelief, sorrow and surprise, when Mark's voice startled him from the barn doorway. 'George, George, my dear friend, I am so sorry this has happened. Luke was angry I had no more money for him yesterday so he took all the horses, leaving only old Molly here. He said she probably wouldn't reach town alive anyway. It's all there is my friend, all there is and nothing anymore to be done about it.'

'Never you mind sir, not your doing, we'll care for her, make the best of it as we always have,' George assured, as he released the tether to walk Molly down to the cottage.

Mark held out his hand, George took it and the warmth of fellowship flowed in their veins. As Mark released his grip, George looked in his hand. . . a golden Guinea looked back. 'No need to say anything George, take it for any emergency you might face. It's all I have, I wish it were more, for you were ever a better brother to me than that wastrel drunkard. I wish you all well and tell you, I will never forget you and your loyal service to my father. Goodbye George.'

Outside their humble cottage, Phoebe looked in astonishment at the old horse but young Sarah instantly loved the quiet gentleness of the old grey. They'd never had a horse before.

'I know, I know,' agreed George, 'I know she's old but if we are careful and do our share of walking too, we'll survive. If we stay here we'll starve for sure. We must always make the best of what we have. Come on boys, you can help me harness her in the shafts.'

Their adventure to a new freedom had begun. Most roads in those days were very poor, almost impassable in places. It became fashionable for the rich to improve some important roads and charge people for using them. George chose instead to take isolated and remote moorland tracks for a number of reasons, it would be very many miles shorter, it avoided the levies of toll roads and there would be free grazing for the family's new horse.

It all began well, with the children and Phoebe walking alongside, George leading the horse, encouraging with kind words gleaned from so many years of his trade. After a few miles they left the small tree filled valleys behind and started the steady climb on to the wilds of Exmoor. They stopped only briefly near mid day, for daylight was still valuable in the month of March. The pace was slow and dependant on Molly the horse, each hour would only see them another weary two miles along the ancient tracks.

Then, George smiled and looked back at his despondently trudging family, 'Look there, lady luck is smiling upon us.' He pointed to a small but well situated farmstead ahead and down to the right. It was only a gentle slope to the farm, it looked a touch run down but had all the essentials, running water, sheltered valley, small orchard, an Ash copse for fuel and even a low lying pasture field that could be cultivated. Little Sarah wandered alongside and chatted to her new found childhood friend Molly the grey horse, who ambled slowly on at the perfect pace for the charming six year old. George waved an open hand to the farmer who was struggling with a broken fence. As they approached, they greeted each other warmly, one for the comfort of shelter and the other the comfort of company.

The farmer introduced himself as William Beer and as he did so, a pleasantly smiling plump lady wiping her hands on a cloth appeared at the open farm house door, 'and this is my good wife, Sarah.' And then, after hearing the traveller's story, William Beer insisted, 'You shall dine with us tonight and the barn is sound enough for shelter. . . it looks like your old horse could do with a rest. . . a long rest!' They all laughed, forgetting all their troubles in that brief moment of joy.

The coincidence of two Williams and two Sarahs was not lost on them, it created an impression of kinship, as in those days children were often named after their grandparents. Old Sarah made a fine fuss of young Sarah and the boys sat by the fire with their mother.

George, having seen the needy state of the farm, offered a day's work from him and the boys in return for the hospitality.

'Gladly accepted George my friend, gladly indeed. Sadly we were never blessed with children strong enough to survive their first years. We're getting older now and yesterday I strained my shoulder trying to keep a wayward ewe from jumping that broken fence you saw me struggling with. Sarah's not up to lifting heavy things either!' Old William smiled a knowing smile.

In the two days the Dinnicombe family finally stayed at the farm, situated not so many miles north of Challacombe, they transformed the place, fences mended, wood collected, chopped and stacked, barn hinges straightened and replaced, weeds cut, water fetched, roof patched. It was a hive of activity, a gloriously happy time, but then it was time to leave. George was destined for a somewhat different future.

The morning of their departure, old William the farmer, with his wife close by, spoke quietly and sincerely to George, 'George, you can see the future this farm holds for someone younger, we have no living relatives, no children to take over when we are gone. We would like to offer your boy William a home with us, treat him kindly like one of our own and one day he will be the farmer here.' Old Sarah held her hands together in hope and Phoebe's hidden hand pinched her husband's arm.

George understood the offer well enough. George had already decided what he must do, he could not give up his child as he had once been. 'In my heart I cannot do such a thing, though I feel the kindness of your words and sense your loss as if it were my own. We must move on and leave you with happy memories and a knowing you will not be forgotten. But our destiny lies elsewhere.'

As they gathered at the farm gate, prepared to leave and say goodbye, Old William warned George of bad weather to come, 'Winter's not over yet George, the wind from the East and the colour of the morning's sunrise tell me that it's possible we may have snow. . . the moor is no place for anyone when that happens. You are always welcome back here if it proves to be too hard going.' Their hand shake was deep in the meaning of lasting kinship.

'Don't worry, William, we shall be fine, two days at most and we'll be off the moor and be on the sheltered wooded lowlands,' assured a confident George, a most able man in his mid thirties and with great strength and energy.

They walked with the horse to the top of the slope, only young Sarah hitching a ride on the back, waving her many goodbyes to the dear old lady who'd been like the grandmother she never knew.

William and Sarah Beer stood together as they always had and waved until the cart and all were gone from sight. They walked slowly back to their house, their minds filled with the dreams of what could have been.

The ancient track was still passably visible and in general followed contour lines or ridges. They were making good time until a trial of nature blocked their path in the shape of a small but unavoidable valley. With the reed growth and sphagnum moss that spread some twenty yards or so across the valley bottom, it was the sort of marshy challenge they could well have done without. 'Everybody off the cart, even you Sarah, lift off some of the heavy things and we'll come back for them,' George was still confident it could be done, but oh for a stronger, younger horse. It was almost as much as Molly could do to lift her feet out of the bog, never mind pull the cart, which action only made her hooves sink deeper. 'Come on boys, hands to the wheel spokes, and you too Phoebe,' called George enthusiastically as he heaved at the harness and encouraged Molly to do her best. She was a willing horse and deserved no flogging. The wheels wobbled side to side with their worn bearings and rocked back and forth as the cart teetered on leaving a deep rut. With rests, it must have taken the family a good half an hour to place the cart on firm ground again. It was obvious that Molly was now lame. Experience told George it was probably a tendon in the lower leg, the swelling had already started, she might be able to hobble on for a while but pulling the cart would probably kill her. It wouldn't be the first horse he'd seen broken winded with age and excessive labour. There was little shelter in this valley of mostly grass and dead bracken though it was less windy than on the tops where the east wind was beginning to carry sleet. The sky was that peculiar grey that had the smell of snow.

'Right Phoebe, we must be a good seven or maybe even eight miles on from the Beer's farm, perhaps over the next ridge there may be another. Shelter as best you can in the cart, I'll be as quick as I can to fetch help.'

Phoebe noticed the change in George's voice, she knew he was worried, she knew that they should have heeded old William's warning and now their very lives were in God's hands. Sleet began to fall more heavily as George, collar up and leaning into both hill and wind that now conspired so cruelly against him, slowly clambered from sight. Phoebe prepared the contents of the cart as best she could to make a shelter, she leaned against the woodworm riddled side and gathered her children close, Sarah on her lap and the boys each side, pieces of sack cloth and a sheet of old darned canvas their only protection from the east wind's determined onslaught. The cold, hunting wind howled through gaps in the cart's sides and strips of torn canvas flapped noisily about them.

Phoebe knew only too well the truth of the matter, not all of them would live through this storm, but she reassured the children that all would be well, that their father would not let them down and would never leave them alone on the moor. She knew he would always come back, nothing would stop him.

Molly, now free from her traces and lightly tethered, stood resolute with her back to the biting wind and the sleet that slowly changed her grey to white, there was only one thing she was waiting for and it didn't disappoint. It wasn't long before she sank quietly to the ground, unnoticed, her work forever over.

George reached the summit with failing visibility but sufficient for him to view the surrounding empty moor. In front was another small valley, it shouldn't take him long to cross it and see if here was a farm the other side, or perhaps a shelter wood. He pushed himself harder than ever, his feet numbingly cold through the worn-thin soles of his boots. The touch of cold sleet pained his hands like a burning from the forge, his hands lost so much control he could no longer close a button nor adjust his collar. He knew as well as Phoebe, that they would not all survive this storm but he was not dead yet and he must find help for his family. 'Just one more hill,' he promised himself, and with fading hope, 'just one more hill.'

The sleet then turned to snow, big snowflakes riding the wind towards him faster than galloping horses, almost pretty to watch, practically hypnotising. . . George shook his head from his strange but passing fascination and pressed on.

Meanwhile, back at the cart, Phoebe's mind was in turmoil, what if George did not come back in time, even if he did will they still be strong enough to move? She thought about

Mr. Beer's generous offer to care for her eldest boy, William. Possibly seven miles back to the farm it was, but young William was a strong boy, well nourished and big for his age, he had the determination of his father and the spirit of his mother. She made her decision. Daylight would not last forever, maybe four or five hours left, if William started out now, while still able, with the wind at his back and before the snow deepened he could make a determined one way hike to the farm before nightfall. Phoebe gently lifted Sarah, who appeared to be sleeping quietly now, to one side, she took off her coat and made William put it on, she wrapped him up well and asked him, 'Tell me William, do you think you can follow the way back to the farm?' William was sombre but nodded back in reply. 'Then off you go with my blessing, may God be with you and guide you all the way safe to the Beer's farm,' she kissed his cold forehead, pulled his cap down tight and helped him off the cart. 'Don't you stop,' she said, 'if you are tired you do not stop, you keep going, say hello to them and we send our love.' 'Don't you stop William. . . whatever happens, you must keep going!' she shouted after him.

William turned, nodded again and was gone in an instant, he felt very grown up that his

mother entrusted him with such a journey. . .
he would not fail her.

Sheltered by two coats, with the cold wind at
his back blowing the snow past him, his path
was clearer, his body warmer and his
intention resolute.

Phoebe settled back in the cart as best she
could, already little Sarah the youngest was
sleeping the long sleep, Thomas huddled
closer, his shivering telling Phoebe he was still
alive, she pulled the canvas and sacking tight
around their bodies and quietly prayed, first
for Sarah, then for William, Thomas and for
her brave George, wherever he was, and only
then for herself.

George's mind was confused, he was still
walking but no longer sure in which direction,
for snow had covered the ground and filled
his footprints. He'd long since stopped
shivering and was so tired he desperately
needed to rest. Then astonishingly through
the curtain of snow, like an apparition, came
another man. The other spoke and beckoned
him on. Though George could not hear above
the wind, bemused, he followed the stranger
to a small cob built shepherd's shelter, it had a
simple but adequate heather thatched roof,
and best of all a small fire of Gorse wood

burned at one end. The host explained that he was a local shepherd looking for lost sheep before the blizzard took its icy grip upon the moor. George, unable to recognise his own rapidly worsening condition, replied in a slurred voice, about his family needing help. The shepherd told him of a small farm two miles further east just off the ridge-way track. Though pleased with such news, George again felt extraordinarily drowsy. He took off his big coat to warm it by the fire and promised himself a few minutes rest before pressing on to the farm. Just a few minutes, that's all, it wouldn't hurt. In a moment he fell fast asleep, it never occurred to him that even if he reached the farm, he was still lost, he would never find the cart again in this storm.

It was in that same instant that Phoebe ceased praying for his return. Hope and breath lay themselves peacefully down in the snow with the old grey horse, innocents all to the worsening storm.

George snapped awake keenly, his eyes acclimatised already to the dazzling whiteness about him. Feeling refreshed and comforted, with what he assumed had been only moments of rest, he glanced about him to see the shepherd had gone and the cob walls of the shelter now just snow lined remnants.

George set off with renewed determination towards the farm the shepherd had described, his mind not in any state to question the events of his journey. He reached the farm with seemingly little effort. His hands no longer burned with the pain of cold, his footsteps were light and easy. He reached into his pocket for the one gold coin he had, the guinea Mark had given him. He would use it to buy help for his family. His closed fist knocked heavily on the solid farm house door but it remained closed. Twice more he beat on the door and called out in pity for someone to come. In the great muffled silence of falling snow, the door remained steadfastly closed to his desperate pleas. He could stay no longer, something dear to his soul was calling to him from across the moors. He turned and ran westwards, quickly blending into the deepening and all encircling whiteness. He would never give up, all that mattered to him was out there, lost somewhere in a landscape that more often than not buried its secrets. A terrible sense of loss had captured his spirit, at this instant George knew he could never ever give up.

Postscript.
Date: 2016, the 6th March.

Somewhere out on the wild moors of the Exe, several miles North West of Challacombe stood a part modernised farmhouse. It had been on the estate agent's books for several months. Remoteness and old wives' tales about ghosts had deterred potential clients, but today . . . success.

Fingering the keys of his modern Range Rover in his pocket, the estate agent smiled with satisfaction at the proud new buyers of Ashcombe Oak Farm, 'I just know you'll love this place, especially when you expressed excitement about buying a remote property with a ghost! The previous owners didn't mind either; they told me it's a kindly ghost, possibly that of an old shepherd that is recorded as missing, presumed lost on the moors. Quaintly it knocks on the door of the original part of the farm house if the snow falls deep. Lovely isn't it? When they opened the door there was nobody to be seen and no footprints in the snow. People love these silly old wives' tales, makes the moors more romantic, more interesting, don't you think? Still, we rarely have much snow here nowadays.

Oh, I meant to say, when the previous owners added the new extension they had to lift some yard cobbles and guess what? They found a golden guinea dating back to 1779, most probably dropped by some careless rich chap. Perhaps there's more out there. . . here's hoping for you eh?'

Each winter, whenever snow lies thick on the moors and the wind blows fierce from the east,

George returns, he is ever lost yet ever searching for his family. Sometimes he chances upon the caring shepherd again, in eternity seeking his lost sheep.

**

Did young William, the oldest child, safely reach the Beer's farm?
Did he live happily, marry, have children of his own and inherit the Beer's farm?
We will never know, we can only trust, as did his loving mother at the time.

**

'So do we pass the ghosts that haunt us later in our lives; they sit undramatically by the roadside like poor beggars, and we see them only from the corners of our eyes, if we see them at all. The idea that they have been waiting there for us rarely crosses our minds. Yet they do wait, and when we have passed, they gather up their bundles of memory and fall in behind, treading in our footsteps and catching up, little by little.'

Stephen King
**

Lynmouth

Only Words.

Fleeting summer joys now only treasured memory, a biting November wind picked up from the East. Seemingly it blew right through him, sending its icy touch beyond his tattered winter great coat to grip his bones beneath. . . His heart, as yet unchanged, remained both warm and steadfast.

The undeniable curtain of dusk was fast drawing closed.

At such a time when the darkling arrives and dims nature's light for sleep, he stood in silence, alone yes but not lonely at the far end of the old pier.

The pier was an enduring legacy from the once powerful empire days of Victoria. Despite abundant signs of dereliction and self sacrifice to the elements, the pier still stood courageous and noble, a warrior leaning out into the wilding and all embracing sea.

It was his ritual to stand there every evening at the end of the pier. He had never missed a day, not one day had he missed, yet none if any would ever notice him.

He would stand and look out to sea while dreaming of the love he had been denied in life. He was but a poor man and she, the dutiful daughter of an intensely rich and scheming merchant.

His own impoverished hovel he shared with reluctant rats that weren't that keen on such frugality or the resident cold and damp either. Her home was warm, lavish, grand and spacious, rich with tapestry curtains, sparkling with engraved glass and glittering with servant polished silver.

He had come to realise, if he truly loved her enough, that there could be no other way to keep her always in his heart. To be sure, he knew it would please her father.

He turned up his coat collar and, sensitively fastening the top button that clung uncertainly to its place in life by a couple of worn threads and with the ease and strength of youth he

climbed effortlessly and silently up on to the railings.

He stood only briefly before he fell. He fell to meet the freedom promised him by the ocean.

In the hundred and twenty three years that have since elapsed, he never missed a day. Each and every evening at dusk he returns to the pier and each and every evening he stands, he climbs and falls to seek the freedom that eludes him still.

Perhaps you've seen him.

**

"The feelings we feel are created by the thoughts we think."
**

Lynton and Simonsbath.

Emily's Friend.

You join us one misty September morning in 1894, it's just after seven in the little moor side cottage.

'If she's not ready soon, I won't be taking her to the mill with me,' George said to his wife, Victoria.

She smiled back and pointed to a small window that overlooked a narrow lane and the river beyond. 'Look there George, she's been waiting for you this last half hour. You know how she loves to visit the mill.'

George returned the smile, picked up the neatly packed lunch basket and replied, 'I know, I know. She's found a friend near the mill to play with.'

George reminded his wife that they might not be back till late, perhaps even after dark. . . but, 'everything would be fine.'

A cart hitched to two heavy horses stood in the lane ready to go. Shires they were, powerful, dependable and hard working creatures. George and daughter Emily, aged eight, climbed aboard and set off with a cheery wave. Soon they left the quayside behind and began the long climb that would take them through the wooded valley and on to the desolate moors.

The colours were already changing with the season and the autumn Sun shone warm and bright. The horses plodded steadily onwards, simply taking the moorland track in their stride. All was peaceful and happy. George whispered to Emily, 'Did you know, something is watching us from the hill to our left?' Emily peered at the hill, seeing nothing but bracken and gorse, then that something moved and she saw it immediately. 'Oh, isn't he wonderful? He must be the finest stag on the entire moor.' As the cart trundled on, Emily watched longingly as the great stag slowly faded into the distance. The great stag watched them go.

'Makes you wonder what else could be out there on the moor, just watching us as we go by, us not seeing, never even knowing,' said George, thoughtfully.

It made Emily think too and she edged closer on the wooden seat to her father's side.

As they neared their destination, the landscape began to change once more to wooded valleys. The mill was down at the very bottom of the valley and driven by water power from the small but fast flowing River Erle.

'Remember to keep away from the water, Emily. You must be . . .' George was interrupted before he could finish.

'Yes dad, I know. Be careful, stay away from the water and the machinery. I've been told a hundred times already,' said Emily with a hint of annoyance, 'my friend always warns me not to go any where near it.'

'Sensible friend that,' George thought, 'Emily seems to be well aware of the danger; I'll not mention it again.'

George drove the horses just past the mill building to a horse trough under a great beech tree where they were glad of the shade and cool drink.

'Come on Emily, let's go in and see the miller, then you can find your friend and play, while I help in the mill.' So saying, George lifted Emily down from the cart. They walked away hand in hand, leaving the sound of horses drinking and the shaking of heads and harness behind them.

'Perhaps I'll meet your friend this time Emily?' George asked.

'She'll probably turn up when all the old people are inside,' Emily replied with a touch of authority.

Emily and George entered the old stone building, where they were warmly greeted by the owner, a kindly man called Harry Baker, 'Welcome, George, good to see you again. . . and you too young Emily, how quickly you are growing up.'

'Right, Emily,' said George, 'we have business to attend to. Take the feed bag off the cart and give it to the horses, watch they don't stamp on your feet. Then you can play a while until I call for you.'

The miller called after her, 'You keep away from the water young lady. You keep well away.' He sounded really stern. Not like him at all.

A couple of hours or so later everything was ready for loading. George leaned his head out of the doorway to see where Emily had gone. She was sitting by a pile of logs talking to herself and giggling. He smiled to see his daughter playing so happily on her own. Obviously her friend hadn't turned up that day. It was a shame.

'Come along now, Emily. We must be off home. We want to be off the moors long before sunset.'

As they prepared to leave, Harry Baker the kindly miller pressed a shiny new copper penny into Emily's hand, 'spend it wisely my dear.'

Emily thanked him and with a smile, stepped outside, looking down at her new treasure. 'Lovely girl, your daughter George, reminds me so much of my own.'

As they followed the moorland track homewards, George spoke with Emily about her friend who hadn't turned up that day.

'But she was there dad, Lizzie is always there, I suppose you just didn't see her,' Emily explained. 'Lizzie is a really happy girl, we're the same age and she's the miller's daughter. We always play by the logs and keep well away from the water, which she doesn't like at all.'

George wasn't sure what to believe; perhaps it was just childish imagination. 'Children are like that,' George thought, as he peered about the surrounding moor, wondering what else was out there that he couldn't see but could still see him.

As the afternoon wore on, the air cooled and the mist began to return, Emily sat closer still to her father, he gently flicked the reins and it wasn't long before they were off the moor. Great hooves clip clopped their way along the lane and the crunch of stones beneath the heavy iron rims of the cart wheels brought Victoria to the door to greet them with a smile. They were safely home before the darkness came and with much news to tell.

Back at the mill, work was finishing for the day. Dusk was fast approaching and the miller struck a match to light a lantern. He stopped by the doorway and brushed dust from a stone set in the wall. He smiled quietly with fond memories as he read the name in neatly carved letters,

"In loving memory of Lizzie Baker. . ." He brushed more dust away with his sleeve and now with a tear in his eye, read on.

". . . age Eight years two months, drowned near this place, fourth September 1888."

"So often the real truth is hidden by what we prefer to think."

**

North Molton

Going home again – a young miner's tale.

An autumn darkness arrived unexpectedly early that evening at the little farm cottage. Henry lit the oil lamp before thoughtfully putting the last of their coal on the fire.

"That's the last the world will see of that small lump of coal," muttered Henry under his breath. The significance of loss and coal was particularly poignant to Henry, whose father had been killed in a terrible mining disaster many years previously. "Dust explosion they said," mumbled Henry, reliving the day he heard that sad news, as he watched fleeting sparks of coal dust flash across the dwindling fire.

"What was that dear?" asked Martha, his caring wife of some twenty five years.
"Nothing Martha, just mumbling about the last of the coal. It'll be early to bed I reckon tonight. There's damp in the air for sure," replied Henry, hiding his real feelings once more, for it's what men did back then.

Though born into a mining family, Henry was encouraged by his late father, James Richmond, to seek different employment; something cleaner and away from the near slavery to which miners were still subjugated in Victorian times. Brave men all, and their families too who often were underground with them, brave men all with scant recognition offered by the wealthy mine owners. It seemed it was their lot in life, indeed their fate, in service to the Empire.

Henry had taken his father's advice and moved south to become a farm labourer; he would not see his father alive again. Henry found a fine young woman from the Henderson family to marry; she was a domestic servant and they met at a hiring fair in a nearby market town.

To be honest it was still a poor life but at least it was free of the choking grime of the pits.

Henry and Martha had only one child, a boy they called James. James was an adventurous soul. One of his regrets was being too young to enlist for the First World War, by the time he was old enough it was over thank God. He remained disappointed at having lost the chance to escape the abject poverty of life as a farm labourer. James had watched his parents work so hard for so little. There they were now, huddled by a tiny fire and with precious little food in their bellies to keep them warm and well.

Wind blown rain tapped like an impatient visitor on the small cottage window, as if to make an announcement, but it was James, standing by the mantle's edge, who spoke, "Father. . . Mother. . . I have something important to tell you . . . I have made up my mind and you will not dissuade me."

In the 'before their age' tiredness of their faces, he could see that they already knew what he was about to say. They had often wondered when the day would come, for as with death, come it does.

"In the morning I leave for Scotland, in Lanarkshire they are employing miners to dig for coal. I want to be a miner, like my grandfather . . . I feel it in my blood to do so," he said, trying to make it sound like his only reason for leaving. The truth was, he was a drain on his parents; he was an extra mouth they couldn't afford to feed. He knew that in the past his mother had pretended that she had already eaten earlier so that her son could have a meal. He'd seen his father limp and struggle with labouring that was all but beyond his ability to survive. The farmer wasn't a bad man but like most landowners of the time was exceedingly frugal with the wages of servants. The very reason the middle classes could afford them – they were cheap and easily disposable; many would find a pauper's grave on common ground.

Henry and Martha knew they must accept James' decision and the three of them sat by their last fire together and exchanged words of advice, wisdom and comfort.

Later as Martha and Henry lay shivering in a cold and un-comforting bed, their minds savaged by the impending loss of their only son, Martha spoke, "In the morning we must smile and be happy for him though it breaks our hearts, we will give him what ever money we can find and make sure he knows he can come home as many times as he likes . . . and he must write us and let us know how he is . . . we don't want him being a stranger."

Henry hid a deep sigh and said with as much fortitude as he could muster, "we will dear, never fear, we will."

Morning came with lighter rain than the previous night but James had already left. He'd left early so that darkness would hide his tears, tears for the loss of his family and home, for he could watch them suffer no more. It was now his turn to meet the world alone and find his own destiny whatever it might bring. He promised himself that he would return one day, yes, he would find great wealth and return to repay his aging parents for all their sacrifice.

A heavy sadness fell like a great stone upon the little cottage. Every night they would dream of James' return. As the years wore on with never a word their dreams became less frequent, more forlorn but not lost forever, no, not lost forever, surely James will return one day.

James had little except coat, boots and his own dreams to carry away with him that cold, portentous morning, as he sadly but resolutely walked the 13 miles to the Railway station. His ticket was paid for as part of an agreement with the work agents employed by the mine owners but he had to pay it back from his wages. There were a few other men waiting at the station; as the great black smoking steam locomotive pulled in and past the short platform, names were called and those who answered were ushered forward to one of the goods wagons. There was to be no comfort on this journey. The men, now some ten in number excitedly introduced themselves. As the journey wore on, the warmth of their meeting was replaced by the cold and hungry reality of their journey. The wooden boards were cold, the only light was through a small dirty window at one end and the only fresh air from a gap in the door to the coupling landing of the wagon.

After a few hours James could stand on his feet no more and wearily slumped down against the unrelenting timber walls of the rumbling wagon. For a while the mesmerising, steady clickety clack of iron wheels on iron track amused him, until his thoughts were interrupted by a playful nudge on his shoulder.

"Hi mate, my name's er John, John Smith, from London. What's yours?" The voice came from a wiry young man sitting close by, about his own age and with a cheeky grin.

"James, James Richmond, my first time away from home," he replied with a shiver.

"No worries mate, you'll be fine . . . you stick with me, I'll see you're alright," reassured John.

With just a couple of short breaks to take on more coal and water, the train took some ten energy sapping hours to reach a small and dirty station next to a coal marshalling yard.

They were soon jolted out of their dog tiredness by the screeching, rumbling noise of the sliding door and a brutally uncaring shout, "Come on, off ye's get and look sharp about it, I'm soon awa for ma supper. Quick, quick, make haste . . . ," it was one of the mine foremen come to walk them to their lodgings.

All the lodgings and houses were owned by the mining company, if you couldn't work in the mine then you couldn't live there . . . simple as that. Everything was owned by the mining company, which in turn was owned by Sir Hubert Montague De Vasey, one of those families that had owned land ever since the Normans invaded. He wasn't a man inclined to visit his mine, his estates in Surrey kept him amused enough.

James, along with John and five others were put up in what looked like an old inn from the outside but inside it was very spartan, wooden boards, big rough dining table with benches and stairs that went up to a number of equally spartan tiny and scantily furnished rooms . . . their new home.

A little old lady, Helen McLeod her name, a pleasant enough soul but with a voice that commanded instant respect, brought them to attention, "There's clean water in the wash basin in your rooms ... keep it like that, I'm not your mother and I'm not here to act like her. The bedding should be clean. . . keep your dirty boots off it and keep it that way, it won't get changed for a month. Breakfast is at five . . . don't worry, you'll hear the bell, even the devil himself could hear it. The well is out the side of the hostel, toilets at the back of the yard, you can have a hot bath for two pence in the laundry room by the kitchen. Don't burn all the candles, when you need more you have to buy them yourself at the mine shop."

James wondered if she was ever going to stop giving orders and if at all he was ever going to remember them, it was so much easier back home . . . he almost wished he were back there already but John timely slapped him on the back and said, "come on James, race you for the best room in the house."

Mrs McLeod was right about that bell, "It must be being rung by someone already deaf," thought James as he eased an aching body out of bed and splashed some cold water on his face. By the time he was downstairs several of the resident miners had already finished their porridge. Mrs McLeod put a bowl in front of him and threw a great ladle of sticky porridge into it, some of it seemed reluctant to leave the safety of the ladle but with a hefty shake it landed solidly in the bowl. James was starving, he'd had nothing to eat for more than a day, and he was so looking forward to the sweet taste of porridge.

"Yuk", James thought as he screwed up his face, and much out of character angrily demanded, "Who's put the salt in my porridge?" Even Mrs Mcleod laughed, they all laughed; it was one of the few laughs they ever heard again.

It being their first morning they were to visit the company stores where they would be kitted out with suitable clothing and instructions. They had to pay for this too, nothing was free, only the air they breathed and for many a poor soul there was eventually a terrible price to pay for that too. Unsurprisingly James had no money of his own but the agent, for a small undisclosed commission, had arranged for James to pay his debts directly out of his wages. The miners were one very short step from slavery; many would be hard pressed to tell the difference. Their camaraderie, sense of purpose and personal achievement was mostly what sustained them, that and the spirits of ancestors who'd walked the same path.

"Ye'll no be wearing they boots down this mine laddie," said the burly store man, pointing accusingly at James' boots.

"But they're all I have sir," James replied apologetically.

"Well, they're no use here laddie, do you want to kill us all? The nails on the soles laddie . . . sparks and gas dinnae mix. I have some old boots o'er here, come and take a look, see if any fit ye." The store man ushered James over to a shelf upon which several pairs of second hand boots looked back hopefully at him.

There was a pair there that looked just right, they called to him from the shelf, it was without doubt they that chose James, not he them. They fitted fine, in fact they felt fine, better than James imagined someone else's boots could feel.

"Aye, a fine choice laddie, a grand pair of boots, they belonged to the late 'Sad Tam' you'll find his name written inside, you can change it for your own later. That'll be five shillings on your company bill." "Next!" he shouted, "Come along lads I've not all day."

James was blessed with an easy day, his mentor, an old miner he only ever knew as Danny and who had something of an Irish accent to him, told him to make the most of it as it would be his first and last easy day at the mine. Danny was to show James the ropes so to speak, where he must go and how he must act, to what work he would be put and the key safety rules he must obey. They both ate that day at the lodging house, which James had noticed often seemed to serve meals for many of the miners even though not actually lodging there.

"Tripe and tatties again James, we get a lot of that .... On special days it might be good beef mince, turnips and tatties, that's a lovely dinner, we look forward to that to be sure," Danny said, wiping his sleeve across his mouth, "I see you've a fine pair of boots James, are they yours?

James looked down at them proudly, then across to Danny, "Yes, they are now, five bob they cost, I think I'll not be seeing any wages for months at this rate. They have 'Sad Rab' written inside, did you know him?"

"To be sure I did, everybody knew Sad Rab. His real name was Robert, he had no other name we knew of, neither I suspect, did he. He was an orphan and joined the mining as a boy; he had no bad habits, no drinking, smoking or other wild pursuits, he was careful with his money, as you can tell by those fine boots you wear today. He always wanted a family, the family he missed so much. He was a good man and his name belied the kind and warm hearted soul that he was, we all liked him and wished he could fulfil his dreams . . . as we'd like to do with our own too." Danny continued, "I can see in your eyes, you want to know if he found his family. Well it wasn't ever to be; Rab was killed in a roof fall about a year ago . . . that's nothing special by the way, for the mine is full of the souls of accidentally killed miners. Look, you can see the scuff marks down the heels of his, I mean your boots, where they dragged him out. He was a good man and you couldn't walk in a finer man's shoes. He'd be happy for you, to be sure."

Life was hectic for James for several months as his body and mind slowly became attuned to the strenuous labours of mining work. Mostly he was just labouring at the beck and call of the experienced men. He was stuck on all the worse shifts that older men avoided wherever possible. "It's the way of it I'm afraid, Richmond," explained the foreman one day, "it will change eventually, vacancies will appear for one reason or another and new miners will arrive . . . then it'll be their turn but until that day you're stuck with the shifts you're given." The foreman was sympathetic enough but an authoritatively stern man; he appreciated that James was a likeable and conscientious worker and should do well in the future; James would just have to learn patience.

The seasons and months rushed by with nary a thought from James of going home, he was now far too busy.

He'd soon made good friends with John from London who he'd met on the train. John, though always somehow behind with his debts, couldn't be described as a trouble maker though it frequently sought him out. About a year or more into their service, John persuaded James to go with him and a few others drinking in the nearest town. It didn't suit James really as he was just clearing his debts and had begun to save money for his dream trip home. He thought of his parents and how pleased they'd be with what he had achieved, him standing on his own feet . . . making his own way in life, yes they'd be proud of him. Not being a drinker by habit the drink went straight to James' head and it wasn't long before John, his so called friend, had talked him into buying drinks for all and sundry. The next day while feeling very much the worse for wear, James was a very remorseful man when he felt in his now empty pockets. He knew that he'd not get home again for a good while yet. . . he must save again. He had a faint recollection of some sort of brawl at the pub but he himself had no marks to show he was involved. At breakfast James saw the evidence of trouble all over his friend's face and hands. John dismissed any questions out of hand, "'twas nothing, I've been in worse, they might well be sorry they picked on me, that's all I'm going to say."

A few days later when John didn't appear for breakfast or lunchtime, James asked if any one had seen him about. It was Mrs McLeod who spoke, "I think we've seen the last of yon young John, the Polis took him away in the night. Not your local Bobbies either . . . all the way from London they were. They said John wasn't his real name and they'd been looking for him for some time. Just his fate eh, he's obviously been a very naughty boy and now he's been called away to pay for it."

James felt some sympathy for his taken friend, for no matter what he may have done in the past he'd been a good friend to him, James only knew the good in him . . . cheeky as he was; Must have been something serious, mind. They never heard any more, it was as though John never was and in any case soon another would take his place. It was simply the way of the world they inhabited.

Months turned into as many years and still James never made it home. Sometimes he felt he'd been away so long that should he return he would find his parents angry with him. The longer he stayed away the more guilt he felt. It almost became easier to mindfully abandon his parents and never think of going home, he felt ashamed that he had abandoned his family so.

James worked hard and saved as much as he could but fate transpired against him to spend it on a journey home. Once it was spent on maintaining the rent on his lodgings after an accident damaged his hands and he could not work for a few weeks. Nobody was allowed to live in a miner's house without being a working miner, widows and their children weren't immune from eviction either, for no profit was ever to be made by such charity. Nobody said life was fair.

Sad Rab's boots eventually wore out and James bought another pair; they were just ordinary boots not like Rab's. He'd thought most often of his parents and home when he wore those boots, the new boots had no such effect but until his feet had broke them in, they gave him many a blister; so much so he began to wonder which was actually being broken in, those boots or his feet.

Sometimes all James knew was the dark. The dark of night and the dark of the pit blended seamlessly into one, especially in the winter. The pit was relatively warm; sometimes he reckoned it was warmer than his lodgings. The pit was not without its moments of fear for James, though in general he was lucky. However, the accident that damaged his hands brought the occasional nightmare to his sleep. After an unconnected incident in the same mine, the fear became a reality and he was awake to it, oh so wide awake. They were part of a rescue team to reach miners the other side of a roof fall and the gap they had to squeeze through seemed to James like some evil unrelenting beast that sought to trap him and grip him underground until he could breathe no more and he turned to bones. James remembered how he had anxiously hesitated and another miner had taken the lead and gone first, making it through the dark, twisted gap to shine his safety lamp back through. The first miner was a bigger man than James and so he knew he shouldn't get stuck – but still frightening none the less. James would ever carry a tinge of guilt for his self presumed cowardice. James had great respect for his mining colleagues, they were a tight knit community and they looked after each other like a strong family. In fact they seemed to have become his family. When asked when he was going home, he always said perhaps this year, but the years rolled on inexorably. Sometimes just before sleep, "I must go home, I must go home," he would say to himself, "I wonder how you are Mother, are you both well?"

In the morning though, it was back to the routine world of work and survival.

Now was the year he intended to go, "I'm definitely going home this year, perhaps in the autumn, yes it's home for me this year," he told his pals one winter breakfast time.

"You see that you do boy, you see you do," Mrs McLeod admonished him, "your mother and father must think you're past dead by now, this year you make sure you go and see them … time to go home boy."

"That's telling ye laddie, ye'd better make sure ye go this time, James," said one of the old timers, stoutly slapping James' back and raising a black dust that slowly settled on table and porridge alike.

"Will you help me write to my mother, Mrs McLeod? I'll go home to see them this year. . . I'll let them know I'm coming," asked a newly excited James. It would seem that having made a firm decision, the weight that had played on his mind was lifted, he felt good about his choice, very good.

"That I will, James. Remind me later and we'll put pen to paper for your mother," replied Mrs McLeod, who had taken a liking to this worthy young lad over the many years he'd stayed at her lodgings.

One of new recruits to join the mining village, the unfortunate soul, was to bring with him the inevitable seed of disaster, a terrible disease of the times. It wasn't long before the few contacts he had made went down with a debilitating sickness. Typhus, rumour said it was; however, the mine was kept open and the miners kept working, they had targets to meet and their wages depended upon reaching them. After about a week, James also began to feel unwell himself and took to his bed, to be fair he didn't take to it but one morning he just couldn't find the strength to get out of it. He was to weaken rapidly and within a few days was reduced to a very sorry state indeed. Mrs McLeod had a word with the visiting doctor; a well liked fair and honest woman, she was on good terms with all. The doctor examined James and concluded that it was probably typhus he had, chances were, him being a strong young man, he would recover.

"He may well pull through on his own Helen," he spoke quietly at the doorway, "I'll leave you some Laudanum for him, it will ease any pains, I'll call by tomorrow. I would keep it quiet a while, for I know the mine owners want any sick miners unable to work to be gone. We'll see how he is tomorrow, must be away now, God bless you for your kind heart Helen."

"You too Doctor, you too," she said clasping the small bottle in both hands, "thank you Doctor, thank you."

It was early evening before the doctor returned the next day; James was deteriorating and drifting in and out of a delirium, whether from the Laudanum or the fever we'll never know. He could no longer see but could hear occasional voices, sometimes he felt there was a woman's presence, he thought of his mother. In his mind he was going home. In his mind he was at the little cottage door calling for his mother.

"Sorry, Helen, nothing more I can do, the company won't pay for his treatment and want him away. I have persuaded them in their own interest to arrange transport to the isolation hospital at Browick Glen, two stops down the track. They will tend to his needs there. Does he have family?" the Doctor's voice was caring and solemn.

"Oh dear, yes," jolted by a guilty memory, "we were supposed to write a letter to his mother one time, I clean forgot, only James knew the address mind, so I'll not be able to write for him. Oh my goodness and he was going home this year too. . . ," she said mournfully.

"You've done your best Helen, nothing more you can do now, it's almost over, I'll make arrangements for the morrow . . . you get some rest too," and with that he turned and left for home.

For James what was left of life, if you could call it such, was quite weird and wonderful, possibly the drugs the doctor had so generously left or perhaps the delirium caused by the fever. Sometimes he thought he heard voices, sometimes he thought he was flying and could see himself from above; sometimes he fleetingly saw people, not always clearly and afterwards could not recall who they were. If indeed he ever did know them. It was time he went home. In fact he knew he was going home, he felt the cold outside air on his face and smelled the coal smoke and steam of the locomotive; he heard the mesmerising clickety clack of iron wheels on the familiar iron track. In his own mind, the journey home had begun and how so very much he looked forward to seeing his mother and father. James smiled peacefully as he felt again like he was floating on air, so much easier than that awful journey away from home up to Scotland, he thought, 'so much easier.' At this point in time he was being stretchered from the station at Browick Glen to the isolation hospital's wagon. "Never seen one in such a state with a smile on their face before," uttered the orderly to his companion.

"Nor I", came the reply, "from the doctor's note we'll be as well to forget the hospital and take him straight to the graveyard." They both smiled the smiles of men with tough jobs to do but who countered their pain with a humour that few on the outside would ever understand.

James felt the floating sensation again as he was lifted to the wagon, then the weight of blankets to keep him warm.

To James the steady rocking motion of the wagon, the clip clop of horse's hooves and the crunch of iron rimmed wheels on gravel were just a short and happy carriage ride to the old farm and home.

Meanwhile down south, at the farm labourer's little cob and thatch cottage, darkness was to arrive unexpectedly early that evening. Henry lit the oil lamp and thoughtfully put the last of their coal on the fire. Martha Richmond stared at the rain-dropped darkness of the small window pane and for one wild moment she imagined she had seen a gaunt unshaven face beckoning her. It made her suddenly think of James, the beloved son she had prayed for every night since he'd gone away and it made her wonder out loud.

"I just know he'll come home Henry, a mother knows these things you know. . . he will come home, something tells me he'll be home," she spoke softly with a certain air of prophecy in her voice.

"No use you staring out that window any more Martha, I fear we will not see him again, God bless him. For all we know he could be dead. If he weren't we'd surely have heard some news from him by now," said a more stoical Henry, doing his considered level best to comfort his grieving wife.

Henry closed the wooden shutters to the other world beyond the glass and lit the oil lamp. They both sat close by to their dwindling fire, "Not much coal left dear," said Henry, as wind blown rain tapped feverishly like an eager but unheard visitor on their little cottage window and a dispossessed wind howled a timely lament under their door.

Footnote:- *The end; for us as much as it was for them.*

While James' spirit had pleaded to his mother through the rain pattered window, the wagon arrived at the isolation Hospital doors and his body succumbed to the inevitable. As much as his body would never return to the little farm cottage his spirit would never return to his body, for now his spirit had no home. Even to this day when the dark and wind blown rain is at hand he still taps on the window of the little cottage, notwithstanding it has now stood empty for some eighty years or more.

**

"Destiny comes not through chance
but by choice.
You are your own destiny."

Pilton

Is it the drum or the drummer that lives on?

Susie was in her mid to late forties I suppose, although she had an ever childlike sense of adventure which constantly led her to seek out all manner of alternative lifestyles and therapies.

Susie's patient and contented older husband, Daniel, a retired police inspector, often joked that it must be in her blood and that in previous lives she was a witch – probably burnt at the stake too. He repeated this to her one day when she returned from a past life regression session she had just had as a birthday treat. Dan didn't mind her peculiar interests, they did nobody any harm. If they did, of course it would be different, very different.

"Well," she smiled, arms in mock akimbo, "it wasn't like that at all – well, not quite anyway." Susie continued, "Some of the things that came up have raised my interest in my own past, you know, ancestors and the like. You could help me with that Dan; it would be easy for you. . . Now, how would you like a nice cup of tea and a big slice of carrot cake?"

Dan laughed, to be sure his younger wife kept him entertained as well as on his toes. "We'll start tomorrow, just you be prepared to find witches somewhere back there! . . . now where's my tea?"

Due greatly to his previous employment, Dan was an absolute ace at tracing the family history, he was logical and methodical in maintaining accurate records and he kept an open mind about any possibilities that others might miss. Despite both Susie's parents having passed away and creating a difficult starting point, in less than two weeks he'd mapped out a chart of Susie's family tree, including lots of intriguing extra details extracted from certificates and census returns. One evening he called Susie to the kitchen where the impressive chart laid spread on the table.

"There", he said triumphantly and tapping with the point of his trusty retirement gift pen on a name he'd written a little way up the page, "this is what you need, a living relative that might tell you first hand of your past."

Susie looked at him bemused; she had long thought any family was either dead or had emigrated into obscurity.

"Yes Susie, this lady here," tapping the name again, "is your great aunt Evelyn, and this is her address. Amazingly she doesn't live too far away. Why not give her a telephone call on this number and see if she'll meet with you," a very satisfied Dan put down his pen with a smile and a flourish and handed Susie a neatly annotated slip of paper.

Susie, lost in thought, held the piece of paper close to her heart for nearly an hour before she made the call. Once contact was made, it was as though they had known each other all their lives, in a moment's meeting, two total strangers had melted together as of one mind.

"Oh, Susie dear, you must be Helen's little girl, how lovely to speak with you, you must be all grown up now. You must come and visit as I can't get about as much as I used to you know. I'll have something special waiting for you."

They arranged that Susie would visit the very next Saturday afternoon, "It's the last house in the cul-de-sac, I'm afraid the paintwork needs doing . . . it's the big house on your right with attic windows . . . I'll leave the front door open for you," Evelyn explained.

Saturday came soon enough and on Susie's insistence Dan joined her. Just as Evelyn had said, the large old house looked worse for wear, as did the garden; Dan could see that no work had been carried out for many years; he hoped that Evelyn was still able to live comfortably inside.

In a back room, brightly lit through large sash windows, they sat on oak dining chairs around a finely varnished oak dining table on which Evelyn had placed various items of family interest.

"Could you bring the tea through dear?" she said to Dan, pointing towards the open kitchen door, "I'm afraid I'd drop it if I try."

Evelyn still had all her marbles so to speak, but was somewhat frail now and hadn't slept in the upper floors for many years. As they settled down around the table with their tea, Evelyn showed various documents that she'd inherited, she and Susie shared the same ancestors and the common bond was overtly tangible.

"You'll be interested in this chap, Susie dear," Evelyn grinned, sliding across a sepia photograph of an eccentric professor like gentleman who appeared to be posing in an antique shop.

"Was this his shop then, Aunt?" questioned Susie.
"Why, no dear, this was taken in his house – he was a great collector of all manner of extraordinary objects. . . some of them quite

strange to be sure. He was a well travelled man and at one time worked for one of the great universities – that is until peculiar things began to happen, then they retired him . . . stress they said it was . . . gave him a small pension. Nevertheless, I think they were increasingly uncomfortable with him rambling on about voices he heard in his head. Well, I mean, nobody else heard them, did they? He was a nice man, Hugh was his name and he'd likely be an uncle to your own grandfather." Evelyn stopped suddenly to listen. They'd all heard it, it was a sort of bumping noise, not easy to describe.

"Perhaps that's him now," joked Dan. Evelyn smiled at him, "No, I don't think so dear, that happens a lot, I think it's a loose window or door upstairs and it knocks when the wind blows, I've not been up there for years now and can't even remember the last time I was in the attic."

"I'll check it out before we go Evelyn, just make sure it's all safe and secure for you," promised Dan with believable authority.

"While you're up there dear, would you do me a great favour? Before he died, Hugh left me an item that he said should be passed on. On no account was I to either throw it away or give it to someone outside the family. Mind you, it didn't come from our family in the first place. It was one of his special collectables from a trip he made to Canada. Being a strange chap, in the nicest possible meaning of the word of course, he quickly made some good friends who were descendants of the Native American community. They were Shamans or something, whatever that means, of the Dakota tribe. . . or at least I think that's what he said. I haven't any children Susie, you are my only living relative and I'd like you to have it. No, it's much more than that, I think that you were always meant to have it, don't ask me why."

Evelyn certainly liked to talk but Susie and Dan were enjoying it – for them this was all exciting stuff.

"So what is it I should look for?" asked Dan.

"Silly me, of course, I didn't say, did I? I must be getting daft in my old age. It's a thinnish hide covered drum, bigger than a dinner plate and has a faint image of a wolf and full moon on the front. . . I think at some time Hugh wrote some words on the back. It's very dusty up there, you be careful how you go." Evelyn was still talking as Dan left the room to explore his way to the attic.

Dan carefully checked all doors and windows on the way up to see if they were loose fitting enough to make that knocking noise – none were. The attic was truly a proper attic in the old style; fully boarded out and with plaster walls, it had a number of curtainless casement windows and its well fitting entrance door was reached by a short and sturdy timber staircase.

It was indeed very dusty in the attic and not without a few old cobwebs either. It had the appearance of being at one time a pleasant living room but had slowly descended into use as a storage space. Dan checked all the windows for security, thinking as he did, that Evelyn probably had little idea any more just what was in this old attic. Putting it down to his old police instincts, Dan was drawn to a chest of drawers covered by old blanket over in the far corner. On investigating further Dan realised there was something under the blanket and, lifting it carefully, was thrilled to find what he'd been sent to fetch, the drum. It was in much better condition than he'd expected, in fact, it seemed as though someone had been looking after it for all those years. As Dan picked up the drum he couldn't resist giving it a couple of gentle taps with his open hand. He knew immediately that Susie would fall in love with it at first sight. With a final and confident check of the door as he left, Dan returned with both excitement and anticipation to the drawing room downstairs.

"We heard you find the loose door, which one was it?" Evelyn asked.

Dan just nodded and told her that they were all fine now and he doubted she'd be hearing the noises again.

Susie didn't notice any of the conversation at all; she was completely captivated by the drum, it seemed that spirit and imagination were connecting her to it . . . and the art work, well, how beautifully done, if the wolf and the moon didn't look real enough then Susie didn't know what did.

As they stood at the front door step with hugs and goodbyes, a shaking and frail Evelyn explained how fortuitous their meeting was, "Don't ask me how or why I think this but I believe you were meant to have this drum and that somehow all those years ago Hugh knew that you would find it through me one day. You found me just in time too as this house has become too much of a burden and soon I'm moving into a nursing home, not sure exactly when. . . the doctor is organising it. I'll let you know what happens. God bless you both and safe journey, enjoy the drum won't you. . . remember what Hugh said."

They waved from the car windows and drove slowly away with some now very mixed feelings about the visit, joy at the meeting, excitement about the drum and worry about Evelyn's health. They were never to hear from her again, only to read about her in the obituary column. . . that was a sad day; A quiet day for reflection on their short but poignant encounter that would change their lives forever.

Sadness couldn't last though, not while Susie had the drum. She'd tried to read Hugh's writing on the back but time had faded the ink, Dan also tried, "Sorry Susie I can't read it either, I'm afraid it's destined to be as much a mystery as Hugh himself."

Several months later, Susie had discovered much about the drum; it was like a portal into a dream world of another reality.

"Not going to your Yoga thing tonight, then Susie?" enquired Dan as he prepared for watching a European Cup match on TV later that evening.

"No, they don't understand what I've been saying, they're too backward thinking now for me," she replied, "I've told them about the messages I hear from the drum and they act like it's silly, like it can't be true."

"That damned drum," thought Dan trying not to show it but he'd had just about enough of it himself, "no wonder she can't go to any of her groups anymore. . . I'm fed up with her ramblings myself."

"Perhaps you should just keep the drum and your dreams to yourself at the meetings, Susie," advised Dan.

She snapped back sharply, "don't you start either," and stormed off to the other room to play the drum for guidance.

Whenever she beat the drum she entered a strangely spiritual but yet more earthy and mesmerising world, a world of far off places, mystical people, wild nature and voices; voices that had messages for her. Sometimes she would hear another pair of hands playing the drum at the same time as she, but the other player was so much better, more emotive, more spiritual more like the drum was speaking its wisdom in its own language. On occasions in this other world, she saw the old white wolf loping in the moonlight to the edge of a camp site, smoke drifted from the tepees quietly into the night sky to join the camp fires of the ancestors. Her fingers would beat the drum yet she would feel nothing, it was as though she wasn't there . . . her body was still in the room but her spirit had already gone elsewhere. She knew in wakeful moments that she lost awareness of her body because consciousness had left it. It was so exciting, it made sense of all she had learned before but at a level deeper than any of her old teachers could ever have explained. She would never let the drum go. . . she was certain that now she knew just how Hugh must have felt, sometimes she even thought she sensed his presence. At times, when the wolf would visit the Indian camp, she became aware of herself calling out to it in a strange language . . . "Anaahey, anaahey," she would cry to the old white wolf; it seemed so right to welcome a friend in such manner. So many times she sensed that she had become a wolf, she knew how it felt to stand in a wolf's body – how else could she know this?

Susie initiated these amazing experiences by first entering a quiet place in her mind and allowing her hands to beat the drum in whatsoever fashion they would chose for themselves. Many times Susie realised that the skill of the drummer was coming through her and not from her – it was a skill far beyond her conscious understanding and ability. At times the drum beat sounded to her hearing mind like the thundering hooves of some great beast with pounding heart carrying her spirit on some mystical errand in a far off land and time.

The white wolf did not always appear but the more Susie beat the drum and entered the spirit world the more she saw patterns emerge. The white wolf often appeared at the edge of the camp in winter and each time during that season's full moon the white wolf and companions would howl their song of hunger. By now Susie knew for sure that the spirit people she was joining were shamans, just as there were many things that simply became 'known' to her – they knew what it felt like to be the wolf, to run like the wolf, to think like the wolf. They knew how every effortless muscle felt, when they rubbed their necks on a tree they felt the fur on bark – their spirits, being one with the wolf, knew no fear. Her spirit left her body and she hunted the snow clad timber line for deer with the pack – there was no telling reality from dream world, each place had its own sense of being and truth. When Susie returned to her body, she knew where she had been . . . the knowing was still with her, so much so that even when fully conscious and aware she could still sense the powerful connected movement of the wolf's muscles. How else could she know how a wolf ran, if she hadn't been one?

As the years wore on so did the strain on their relationship and eventually Susie and Dan agreed to go their separate ways. He moved back to his home town and Susie stayed as she was.

Dan plodded on in a simple life of retirement and he renewed old acquaintances from the force. One Christmas he was invited to a reunion party . . . "How's the lovely Susie?" an old friend asked.

"Long story," Dan replied, "short answer is I don't know. She became fixated, addicted almost, to some sort of cult like thing – just needed to go her own way. It's a great shame but there are no guarantees in life old pal."

"Only the one," added his friend, smiling, "only the one," and patted Dan kindly on the shoulder in sympathy.

Meanwhile, as the years sneaked by, unnoticed until they were well past, Susie continued to discover more and more while on her out of body journeys. It was beyond her understanding why others weren't queuing up to do the same; it wasn't as though she'd kept her discoveries a secret, just that people didn't seem to want to know. Susie lost all contact with the therapy community which she had frequented so much before and she spent more time alone, though not spiritually alone of course. At one point she'd been writing engaging articles for a holistic health magazine under the nom-de-plume of 'Moon Wolf'. As her writings (or wild ravings as the editor began to view them) became more intense, the magazine refused any further submissions from her. Susie began to spend more time talking to herself, her drum and the spirits that visited. Susie had never studied Canadian history or that of the First Nation peoples but now she knew so much of it, the knowledge just seemed to turn up, much like finding hidden treasure in the attic of her mind. Much of what she knew was never of the written word but came from fable and song. She just seemed to 'know' without looking or asking.

She knew all the stars where ancestors had found a greater peace from an ever alienating world. She knew about the Moon, its influence on intuition and how it guarded the earth while the Sun rested. Susie knew all of this, but not a word of Dan's passing; he who'd shared the joys in life and had been so instrumental in Susie's fate.

As the years steadily grew into decades, Susie's house and garden also began to fall into decline and she spent ever more time visiting the spirit world while her earthly body became increasingly frail. One day, she picked up the drum and turned it to look on the inside; it wasn't something she'd ever been bothered with before as the wolf and the moon were far more alluring. By now Susie had no contacts in the 'normal' world and not one living relative of whom she was aware, she'd abandoned the family history research when she found the pleasure of the drum . . . now she was alone. To Susie's great surprise, Hugh's writing and some hitherto unnoticed strange symbols were becoming clearer, the older and more frail she became the clearer the writing. Finally, using her reading glasses and in good light, she could at last read Hugh's message.

'I have at last deciphered the ancient symbols, they foretell a mystical journey. A journey entirely of your free will but you must confer the drum to another before death summons you. Failure has grave consequences. When my writing becomes clear enough to read, please hurry, you will have little time left.

May the spirits be with you, Hugh.'

Hugh's writing finally delivered its stark but belated warning. As so often happens in life, a warning which often condemns us to wander a path we had mistakenly chose to follow. The wonders of hindsight arrive too late to serve us well in our time of need.

However, Susie did try to find another who would accept the drum as their own but without success; in part she didn't want to be free of it, its hold too strong for her weaker will.

Susie reflected on her dilemma, could she ask the old white wolf? The white wolf symbolised intelligence, leadership, family and strength; the white wolf also epitomised perseverance and intuition. The question was, "Where were these in her, what was she doing wrong?"

Susie was more familiar with the ancestors around their starlight camp fires better than she knew who ran the corner shop down her street. She knew the life of bear, eagle and deer better than she did her neighbours of more than thirty years. She actually liked it that way.

Late one cold winter's evening at the time of the full moon, Susie was not feeling very well, she had been ailing for a while but now the pain in her chest and joints was becoming intolerable. Susie chose to leave her pain racked body behind and visit the spirits through the drum's mystical portal. She placed lighted candles about the room, drew the curtains and turned off the electric light, then she settled into her comfortable chair and began her ritual.

As she arrived at the spirit camp she noticed it was more crowded than usual, as though the shamans were gathering for a special occasion, there were many camp fires and several faces she had not seen before. Looking up she could clearly see the full moon, seemingly smiling down on her like a long lost sister just found. The camp was surrounded by a low lying evening mist among the nearby Alders and Maples. As she peered into the mist she saw not one wolf but two, one light, one dark. As her eyes grew accustomed to the mist she saw the great grizzly bear and the black bear too . . . oh, and deer present in plenty; at their head was a great and noble stag, an ancient looking beast of wisdom with a greying white coat. Susie became ever excited as the mist further revealed what it so recently had concealed. The mists for Susie were clearing; the camp was circled with the benevolent gaze of animals and spirits, all looking on in expectation.

An elder and obviously revered shaman beckoned her to sit with him at his fire; she sat next to him sensing the welcome he offered, they warmed their hands by the light of the burning wood and watched the sparks of life slowly rise and abandon the fire for another place. As the heat of the fire seemed to warm her very soul, the old shaman told Susie the often celebrated tale of the two wolves, one good, one bad. They were opposites in the universe, as must exist for all things and for all time; they would fight each other until the strongest won.

When Susie asked which wolf won – the answer came, 'the one you feed.'

A day later a rubbish skip appeared outside Susie's fire damaged house, accompanied by Police tape and a sign that read, "Keep Clear. Unsafe Structure."

Three weeks later, the following appeared in the small ads of the local paper.

Genuine Canadian Native Indian Drum.
Endearing and pretty, you'll fall in love with it.
Vibrant and life like art work depicting
an elderly squaw accompanied by a howling
wolf under a full Moon. Slight smoke damage
hence yours for only £20 or near offer.
A bargain you'll not find again while you live.
Tel **** 656768

**

"Belief gives birth to power."

**

Porlock Weir

The long walk home - *Louisa's* way.
Walking in the footsteps of ghosts.

Way back in 1899, after hauling the Lynmouth lifeboat *Louisa* to Porlock Weir, those not part of her crew returned to Lynmouth with her launching carriage. Now the urgency to save lives was replaced by their simple wish to go home.

On the night of 15th November 2016, I decided to walk that tormenting path myself. There was something out there I needed to know.

In 1899, Jack Crocombe had his plan and in 2016 so did I, and there the similarity ends. However, one aspect remains true of any journey over the moors, if you weaken and falter by the wayside then chances are, you will die out there. A bit melodramatic? Well that's what I went to find out.

At some point, determination becomes desperation and previously noble dreams turn to anxious prayers of hope; it is what you do at this juncture that will decide your fate.

The moon rising over Porlock Bay bid me time to leave. I'd had a hot meal in one of the hostelries and thought on those who braved that January night back in 1899. How many had eaten well that day, how many were hungry from the start? Indeed, how many had said their goodbyes before they left? How many had fine boots to wear, boots good enough for the mud and stones of their path? I thought on those whose boots may have been needing repair, thin soled and leaking. My own boots were good, waterproof and comfortable but by the time I'd climbed to the summit, my feet were calling out to me in misery, as must have theirs. To avoid being run over by modern man in his motor car and prematurely killed on the main Porlock hill, I chose the toll road, which as it turns out, is further, adding a mile to my journey and compensating for my early stop at the Blue Ball Inn at Countisbury.

On reaching that Porlock summit, some five miles in the waiting, I sat by the roadside, where Culbone stables once stood. *(Now a pub, but closed for refurbishment the night I was passing and currently not a pub at all.)* By the light of the moon I changed my abrasive newly purchased so called 'walking' socks for softer more comforting ones. Once more, I thought of those brave men in 1899, tortured by stormy January weather and who had neither such an opportunity nor luxury.

It is a fantasy to think the moor is flat between the two giants of Porlock and Countisbury, undulating, I'd accept. But for tired legs and blistered feet, every slope is a challenge; a challenge to be met . . . and overcome. You cannot give up; there is no one but yourself to turn to for help – you *are* the help. What are you to do? Stop by the wayside and await the inevitable weakening by hypothermia - or plod on, one painful step in front of the next. Though I was blessed by a full moon and clear skies, the earlier villager's journey was shrouded in the total darkness of a new moon, with only oil lamps to find the road. . . when tiny flames weren't being blown out by the gale.

There comes a point in any journey that it becomes less arduous to continue forward than go back, regardless of the difficulties.

Whether taking *Louisa* from, or the carriage back, on the narrow track to Lynmouth, there was little opportunity nor appetite for turning back, they must succeed. For me, I could ask at a farm house to phone a taxi to take me to a hotel. But who in life enjoys failure?

Pride should always be tempered with practicality and shame belongs, not in failure, but in not always doing your best.

As would have they, I kept a lookout in the distance for any welcoming light. Eventually I saw one . . . but my heart sank, for it was a long, long way off and I was beginning to have doubts how much I had left in me – body and spirit alike. As fortune would have it, the lights were from Lynton and my own destination, the Blue Ball Inn, was much nearer, though still hidden on the far side of yet another unwelcome 'undulation'.

Finally as I launched my aching body into my car, my journey now over, I thought on those soaked and aching heroes who launched *Louisa* over the leg breaking pebbles of Porlock Weir beach, into a storm laden sea. Their journey was not over – it had only just begun, the next day, tired, torn clothing, injured or not, they must work to make a living; their struggle never over, never forgotten.

Yet, all I had to do was rest in my car for the pub to open its doors and await the call of a great fried breakfast.

(Now you know all there is to know about the author of these short stories.)

**

"He, who is carried to the temple gate, can never know how far it was."

**

South Molton

An Anniversary Gift from Exmoor.

Jingling a set of anxious car keys in his pocket, the Estate Agent leaned on the hallway newel post, looked up the wide, carpet-less Edwardian staircase and called out, "Yes, lady, the attic does need to be emptied; if you like I can call in a house clearance chap we work with and just add it to the bill for you."

"It's okay," replied Gillian, "I'll do it myself, after all he was my Uncle; I owe him that at least."

The Agent's goodbyes were lost to her ears as Gillian flicked on the switch to a dust covered electric light bulb in the attic. To the strange but distinctive smell of hot dust and old papers, Gillian began to examine her lately deceased uncle's 'treasures'.

For many years her uncle had been a rural journalist in the South West. His quiet non-intrusive nature had earned him much respect and trust, a trust he had never betrayed; his friendly nature had endeared him to the public through whom he sought a living. A good and honest man; now he was passed to the other side and Gillian was determined to handle his estate with justly due respect.

It wasn't long before Gillian became aware of some old diaries and notes from the nineteen sixties; there was something about them that made her want to pick them up and hold them close; it was almost as though she was meant to find them.

Turning off the attic light as she left, Gillian retired to a comfortable sunlit room at the back of the house; it was a room that overlooked a wild but pleasant garden, a garden that seemed to be looking in on her as much as she looked out on it. Gillian sat in a high-backed armchair by the window and placed the papers on her lap. Smiling to herself, she thought, "I bet this was Uncle's favourite chair," and then she began to read.

This is what she found.

Note for file;

Interview with Edward and Alexandra Hilyard, Monday 19th September 1964. Reference a strange and ghostly experience on the moor.

Edward Hilyard seemed a man ever angry with the world yet never so with his dear wife of some forty good years. Alexandra Hilyard was born about the same time as her husband during Queen Victoria's last days in 1901. Alexandra was not a well lady, a victim to a terminal illness she decidedly wished to keep to herself, she suspected this would be her last year. . . she had not told her husband in order to save him from the premature burden of knowing. Edward remained oblivious to the facts; she said it was better this way. This was the weekend of their fortieth wedding anniversary and their trip from the midlands in their old Morris Minor to Exmoor was a special gift to each other in celebration.

As Gillian leafed through the pages of notes, a scrap of paper fluttered floor-wards, she caught it easily in her hand; in a red inked scrawl of forceful and jagged handwriting it read, 'Utter rubbish! This newspaper is not a comic, do not submit any more gibberish of this sort again.' . . . it was signed by her uncle's editor of the day, the pressure of his pen had almost broken through the paper. "Obviously not a believer," decided Gillian as she resumed the fascinating study of her uncle's notes. "Poor old Uncle," she reflected quietly.

Alexandra Hilyard's statement:-

"We were so tired from our long journey but were still excited about staying for the weekend at our hotel on Exmoor. It was late afternoon and a grey mist had descended on some signless and narrow moorland road we had taken. I never was any good with maps, ours didn't show those little roads anyway and we never once came across anyone to ask. We seemed to crawl along blindly for an eternity, the fog was thicker now and soon it was dark too, about half past six or so I think, poor Edward could hardly see the road, the lights on our little car aren't that good you know, he kept to the road by following the verge on the left, it's all we could do, that and hope we'd come to a village soon. . . but we didn't. He said he was worried about the petrol running out, it was getting colder and the car heater never was much good at the best of times. I started to pray for a miracle. . . and then one happened. . . two great stone built gate posts appeared just off the road to the left.

The gravel drive looked good and Edward said it must go to a big house or a farm. He said we should go down there and 'throw ourselves upon their mercy as strangers hopelessly lost on the moor,' he said.

From what little we could see through the fog it was a grand double fronted mansion with a central great door, it was so quaint and rustic with the soft light of oil lamps either side. It looked big enough to be a hotel, we decided to ask if we could stay or at least have directions to help us on our way. We approached the doorway more frightened of the fog on the moors than we were of knocking a stranger's door at night. They had one of those old fashioned bell pull rods that rang a bell by cable, you must know the sort I mean, but they are usually so old they don't work anymore. It wasn't long before the door opened to a very polite young lady with impeccable manners and all dressed in maid's clothing; all in a heavy dark dress to the ground with a white apron and mop cap she was. . . pretty as a picture. She made a tiny gesture like a curtsy and invited us in as though we were expected. "Come on you through to the drawing room sir, we have a warm fire waiting for you," she'd said in a soft Devon accent. Well Edward liked that, I can tell you, not only welcomed in but a warm fire and being called 'sir', that was a first for him I can tell you. She took our coats and insisted we stayed the night, "people suffer miserably and even die out there on the moors in fog like this," she'd said, "you're welcome to stay the night. . . we so rarely see visitors these days. I'll just ask you to be sure to leave early before the young master returns home in the morning. Best to go before he comes home at daybreak as he's been a touch angry these days. . . don't you be telling anyone I said that mind you. I'll fetch you a bite to eat and have your bed warmed for you."

We couldn't believe our luck, what a dear young thing to help us so and what an amazing house it was too. The drawing room was full of grand furniture, large gilt framed paintings adorned the walls, candles burned in Georgian brass candlesticks and a decorative oil lamp, like my grandmother used before she had electricity, reflected light off the highly polished surface of a circular mahogany table. I remember Edward saying that they probably couldn't get the electric so far out on the moor and that it was a good job they didn't have a lot of visitors as, sure as eggs is eggs, all those fine antiques the place was full of would soon be knocked off by burglars if they knew about them.

We sat by the great carved marble fire place with our feet out towards that lovely fire. . . oh, how that fire seemed to solve all our problems.

Our dear young hostess soon brought us both some warm milk, wonderful cheese and pieces of the finest home cooked ham I've ever seen or tasted. As I turned to thank her I caught a glimpse of what I can only guess were deer hounds or something similar. . . great big rough coated dogs, a pair of them, padded silently by the open doorway along the flag stones of the hall outside and towards the main door. Edward was too slow to look up from his plate and see them but he assured me they would be friendly, "throw them a bit of ham if you're worried," he joked with me. I'd not seen Edward so happy with the world for many a year. . . it brought a smile to my face, yet a tear to my heart . . . What with me knowing all what I do and all that. Later that night as we lay in bed, a nice cosy bed it was too, how they warmed it up without electric I have no idea, anyway, as we lay in bed, a night candle burning warmly by our side, we talked of our day and the adventure we had endured and now so enjoyed. Edward said that it couldn't have been a better anniversary gift if we'd planned it this way, it was the very stuff of life itself, he'd said. I began to wonder if the place was in fact a hotel of sorts as I'd seen other guests on the upstairs landing going quietly to their rooms, some dressed in the fashions of various bygone years. I hadn't spoken to them as they seemed to be quite lost in their own thoughts and with everywhere as quiet as the grave I didn't want to spoil their stay. I thought perhaps we'd all meet up and chat at breakfast but as it happened we didn't see them again, for we left just about dawn as asked by the maid. She was such a little sweetie that we couldn't let her down and get her in any trouble with the master of the house. We'd slept warm and safe until it was time to leave in our little car; we thanked God we hadn't stayed lost on the moor. There was a little mist still but the maid said it would soon clear and we would find our way towards town if we turned right at the end of the drive and stayed on the main thoroughfare; she stood on the steps and waved us goodbye with a cheery, 'God speed and safe journey.'

Edward was concentrating on his driving, as he always did, but I saw a frenzied rider approaching the house across the fields, he was riding hard, whipping his lathered horse and with a thunder black look upon his face. No wonder that poor soul wanted us away before his return, I thought. As we passed through the stone gateposts they looked quite different from the night before, they now looked unkempt and almost derelict, had they looked like that when we arrived I doubt Edward would have ventured along that overgrown driveway. I'm not sure if I heard screaming and shouting behind us but what with Edward changing gear and humming some happy song to himself I can't for sure ever say that I did now. On coming to a small hamlet we checked our directions with a couple of hedge layers walking their way to work. When we told them of our lucky overnight stay they were bemused and told us there was no such place . . . they insisted that, knowing the moors as they did, they knew more than us and we must be mistaken! We decided to stay one last night in a hotel in town and the landlord put us on to you to hear of our strange tale. . . . and there, now you have heard it."

Interview concluded 11.30 am.

19th September 1964

**

'Additional Historical Research:-
Note for file-

The remote Wyke Grange, built about 1860 by a family of Lancashire mill owners, burned to the ground with a total loss of life on Friday 18th September 1891. The young owner, a Mr Edward Lightfoot Esquire tragically perished in the flames and this only a day before he was due to marry a local notary. The cause of the fire remains unknown but preparations for a grand weekend celebration are thought to have contributed to the blaze. The fire would have burned unnoticed and uncontrolled for some considerable time; the building was so badly damaged that no bodies or remains thereof could be found for decent Christian burial. (They lay there still and will forever more.) Edward Lightfoot's bride to be refused to discuss the matter when questioned and it was said by a close friend that she had in fact already previously planned to leave the County; she asked for privacy in her grief.'

**

Gillian tried to share her exciting find with many friends but when confronted by continuing disbelief she eventually threw the papers away, never to speak openly of them again. Doubting listeners had always glibly 'explained away' the story with their own superior views; yet none dissuaded her from the honesty of her uncle's judgement, he was an honourable man. She owed him her trust at least.

Author's note:-

Today, any and all remains of the Wyke Grange, including the gate posts and drive, are lost to the moor and gorse. There are precious few records of its short existence. Young Master Lightfoot, a commonly angry man with all the world, suddenly jilted by his bride to be, destroyed

*and burned all about him in a crazed fit of rejection
and madness.*

*The 'guests' that Alexandra saw at the
Grange that night perhaps were other lost
travellers lured in by the gate posts and lamps of
the Grange as they sought sanctuary from the
moorland fog. . . but for some unknown reason
they had not left the house before the master
returned,. . . so condemned to remain forever in a
place that does not exist in real time.*

*If you venture to ask, you'll find those
who work the moors nearby will shake their heads
and deny they have ever seen the old stone gate
posts half hiding in the mist. . . they prefer not to
know. . .not to tell. . . a wisdom perhaps you
might consider yourself.*

**

*"The way you wake up is the way you live
your life."*

**

Westward Ho!

The writer – all souls day.

From childhood, Susan Richmond had one abiding ambition – to be a writer. However, life had conspired to keep her dream out of reach, until today.

Today was All Souls Day and she decided to write a story in honour of her parents, both of whom had been talented writers. Her father was an eminent archaeology professor and author of many great historical novels. Susie's mother was more of a children's story teller - skilled with the sort of beautiful bed time stories that forever remained treasured childhood memories.

Tragically, both parents lost their lives in a house fire while Susie was away at university. She would have been nineteen back then, some thirty years ago. The fire officer's report to the coroner had indicated that her mother was probably dead long before her father had entered the burning building in a desperate attempt to rescue her. A futile but brave effort that would cost Susie both of her parents.

Susie had tried writing stories many times before but any worthwhile tale always proved beyond her.

'None the less, today's the day,' she vowed, 'of all my days this is it. This evening, the magic will begin.'

She'd heard somewhere that a ritualistic scene setting was the key that opened the door to great stories. Such rituals placed the writer's spirit somewhere unworldly, somewhere between heaven and earth, in a twilight zone where souls could exchange ideas.

During the day, she tidied the house until all her jobs were complete and out of mind. She then lay resting on her sofa, listening to Tibetan chants on a CD she'd come across by accident in a charity shop. She waited quietly for evening to arrive.

Susie placed a cushion on one of the kitchen chairs and a small electric lamp on the table. The house was otherwise shrouded in darkness. Then Susie brought out a lavender scented candle, a mug of herbal tea, a glass of red wine, some white copier paper and her best fountain pen with spare ink. She sat comfortably, satisfied that the ritual was as good as it gets, her back warmed by an open log fire. Across the table, she observed her own reflection in a dark kitchen window. As Susie stared thoughtlessly at her own reflection it amused her to see glimpses of her mother and her grandmother looking back. These brief apparitions pleased her, as she remembered those kind people. Susie smiled to herself, took a sip of wine and picked up her pen.

The clock on the wall tick tocked its sleepy song, the full moon showed itself briefly from behind the clouds and the world journeyed on relentlessly.

'Oh no, not again,' she sighed, realising that all she'd done was stare at the white paper. The paper, without judgement or emotion, simply stared back, as it had already done for the last ten minutes.

Anxiously, she stared wide-eyed into an unhelpful gloom and begged the heavens for help. Anyone's Gods would do, ancestors, angels, even the devil himself if they could only release her imprisoned spirit.

Then it arrived, a joyful spark of inspiration. She didn't need anyone's help after all. Indigo ink flowed freely from her pen, though not quick enough for the wonderful ideas that crowded into her mind. She was almost in tears with the hurry to scribble one thought down before the next one pushed it aside. Her pen frenziedly scrawled across page after page. The scented candle flickered benevolently as she reached out for a sip of tea. The fire at her back reminded her of sitting on her mother's lap and the warmth of her body while some enchanting story lured her into the strange world of dreams.

Susie's father had told her more than once, 'a story must always have a grain of truth, like the grain of sand in an oyster from which something beautiful will grow.'

Her own grain of truth right now was about never giving up hope, that everything must be possible if you only apply yourself wholeheartedly into the venture, for it is belief itself that gives rise to real power.

Reflections looked lovingly on from the window pane, the soft light from the table lamp and perfume from the candle flame effortlessly carried Susie's hand across the paper – a masterpiece in the making. In beautiful script, the writer's spirit indelibly crafted the essence of story in her mind – it was no longer a mystery. Her father's words again whispered to her soul, 'Never try and possess something, for it will in turn, imprison you.'

At last, she'd made it. She was completely at one with her story, a mistress of her own destiny. The story was good. No, better than good. It was exceptional and very few alive today could compete with its brilliance. It was a prize winner for sure. Totally original, with heroine, mystery, danger and eternal hope, it was all she'd dreamed of, ever since she could remember.

Finally she put down the pen and felt her body relax. Then, the strangest thing, she sensed her father standing behind her, hands light and kindly on her shoulders, like when helping with her homework as a child. His voice, filled with reassurance, 'There dear, it's not so difficult after all, is it?'

Susie was startled by a burning log falling in the fire place and illuminating the room with its eerie light, her tea was cold, the candle nearly out.

She looked down to admire her work.

Blank white paper looked back, still waiting.

**

'Of ghosts, as it is with mirrors,
only on reflection will you know
what might exist.'
Richard Small

**

Woolacombe

Harry's rescue.

Dave's feelings were more than a little hurt as he recalled his wife Beth wagging a finger at him from the kitchen doorway at home saying, and not without a touch of inherited venom in her voice, 'If you don't go to mother's seventieth, I will be and I won't be coming back!' He knew she meant it too; she'd been the love of his life but was quite difficult to live with for sure. However, he didn't want to lose his home and family and so it was that, one autumn Friday afternoon they arrived at the cosy but fateful hotel on the west coast. The family had clubbed together in a haphazardly unequal way to pay for the special event. Dave suspected that his share was considerably more than his brother-in-law Nathan's. Nathan, an astute and manipulative man, was almost as mean as his mother and had been named after a frequently friendly local family butcher.

Beth and Dave enjoyed a reasonably friendly evening on their own, as they had travelled down a day earlier than the rest of the party. Their room was pleasant and comfortable but without a sea view, as those rooms were reserved for Beth's mother and company. As they settled into the plush bed and put out the lights, Beth warned Dave once more of the consequences of alienating her mother, 'Don't you dare be rude and don't you dare wander off and leave the party. We're only here to give mum a good time for her special birthday.' Both room and mood plunged into an even deeper darkness. Dave mumbled his agreement and turned over with some sadness. He couldn't stand the mother-in-law, he could hardly choke the words out to even speak to her, he certainly never called her 'mum' or even by her first name. He called her Mrs Briarley on the odd occasion he was obliged to converse. Dave was fully aware that his mother-in-law was of the opinion that he was a useless, weird and unpleasant object that would have been better off being put down at birth. She hadn't attended their wedding, had written Dave specifically out of her will and refused to acknowledge Dave and Beth's three now grown up children. None of that bothered Dave as he doubted she had any money to leave and her absence from his life was a blessed and possibly divine intervention – to his way of thinking anyway.

In general, Dave interacted well with most people, he liked chatting to the landlady at breakfast, he enjoyed greeting people in the street and always had sound advice for his children on the odd occasion they might distain to listen. Beth had few friends but wasn't too bothered, they were mostly idiots out there anyway, and especially the man she regretted ever marrying.

The family, various attached partners and their children arrived midday and after a brief exchange of obligatory greetings, went to their rooms to rest. At least that's what they said they were doing.

Dave was at a loose end, he'd read all the hotel's newspapers, perused the paintings on the wall, mulled over the menus a few times and stared out of the window at the sea. And he knew worse was to come! He returned to his hotel room where he found Beth sitting on the bed, filing her nails over his pillow and preparing for the party. 'For God's sake, stop moping about, why don't you do something useful for a change!' she exclaimed, having been quite happy with her own company.

'I think I'll go out for a walk along the beach,' Dave said almost as though asking permission. He suffered a little from a self esteem issue.

'Right, that's it, all my family here and you want to go for a walk on the beach, that's charming isn't it?' she retorted, 'Well go then and be back well before the dinner, you be back by four, or else.'

Dave wondered as he turned the door handle what the 'or else' might be, but was left in no doubt when Beth assured him, 'If you're not back for mum's party then you'll be dying a lonely old man!'

As Dave wandered left along the beach and away from the hotel and edge of town, those words played on his mind, in fact he would never forget them to his dying day. He just couldn't understand how someone could even think such things, he didn't want to be lonely at all, let alone die in that way.

The further Dave walked from town the more he began to relax, the sea air, the autumn sunshine, gulls calling him to look at how well they flew, small grey stone cliffs and a sailing boat far out at sea . . . all compounded to make life so much better, so much happier. Dave checked his watch, plenty of time, he could go another half hour at least before turning back. Just up in front and round a small promontory, he spotted what looked like 1940s war time defences. 'Worth a look, this,' Dave thought, 'this is interesting.' It seemed like there may also have been a small landing pier at some time, though the sea had brought the once proud and staunch metal framework in a tangle to its knees. There was a recent chain link fence with a sign attached,

MoD Property. NO ENTRY. DANGER.

However, there was an easy gap in the fence near the cliff face and it looked like people had made a habit of passing through, 'Perhaps fishermen,' thought Dave as he stood unashamed and excited on forbidden ground. 'This is more like it,' Dave chuckled to himself, 'knocks the socks off sitting down to dinner with the mother-in-law.'

Back at the hotel the family was beginning to assemble in the lounge. Pretentious greetings intermingled with handfuls of free nuts and canapé's.

'Like a flock of vultures they are dear,' confided the landlady's husband. He was sharply rebuked, 'Shhh if they hear you say something like that, they could easily write us bad reviews, they seem that sort. You be on your best behaviour and take 'em some more nuts out. . . I'm helping the cook now with the meal preparations.' 'Oh, and the nice chap who came last night with his wife has gone for a walk along the sea front, said he'd be back before four, keep an eye out for him, poor man.'

By now, a new self empowered Dave had drifted off into childhood dreams and memories and was exploring the remains of reinforced concrete and twisted metal, all of which were unsighted from the town . . . 'and for good reason no doubt,' thought Dave.

The green sea algae had made Dave's new playground more slippery than ice. A disaster was inevitable and not slow in arriving.

'You stupid, stupid man,' his self admonition a mixture of grief and annoyance. . . instead of looking where he was going he'd glanced at his watch. . . he'd fell, twisting his ankle into the bargain. 'Idiot, idiot, idiot,' he said with more than a wince of pain, looking at his only good clothes covered in sand.

'Oh well, nothing for it but brush myself down and limp straight back to face the music I suppose,' but his foot had slipped between the rusty metal lattice and he couldn't pull it back. The more Dave panicked the worse it became and the injury was already beginning to swell his ankle, making extrication nigh on impossible. What was he to do? He was more in fear of his domineering wife's retribution than the more imminent disaster of drowning, a fate incidentally, which did not cross his mind for some minutes. Drowning? Dave looked about him, the tide was out, yes, but it would be coming back. Even if he could sit up he was still below the seaweed that had made its home on the old pier stanchions . . . if he didn't get out he would drown, he was trapped and going to drown. . . slowly and inexorably. Dave panicked even more and began to shout, even scream, for help. He paused to listen hopefully for a reply, surely there must be others out here, fishermen, dog walkers and the like . . . the only sound that came back to his eager ears was the distant soft swoosh of gentle waves on sand and the hungry cry of a seagull looking for something dead or dying on the beach. He checked his pockets. . . his wallet, car keys, a creased up hotel menu and his mobile phone! 'Thank you God, thank you,' beamed a relieved Dave. His fingers fumbled to turn it on, it seemed to be working and there was still life in the battery. He decided to contact the hotel, he really must speak to his wife first. . . she would understand. Then he'd call the emergency services, the coastguard would be best, perhaps the fire-brigade too, and why not an ambulance because that ankle didn't look too good, possibly broken, certainly ligaments gone. Dave used the number on the hotel menu to dial, he had to try twice as his fingers were shaking so much. . . he put the receiver to his ears and waited . . . nothing. He looked at the phone screen, 'no signal'. Dave could have wept, no blasted signal, the one time in his life when he really needed the phone and there was no signal! He tried again and again, trying different positions, holding the phone high, holding it next to the steel work . . . none of it made any difference. Dave tried to sit up so that he could reach his ankle but the angle his foot was pinned meant that his knee would not allow it. There was still plenty of time, the tide would surely take several hours, I mean it only comes in once a day doesn't it? Help would arrive from the hotel long before that. He called out loudly again.

Meanwhile the Briarley clan were gathering in the lounge in preparation for their celebratory dining experience. The guest of honour, a paradoxical accolade, circulated importantly and in her time honoured fashion badmouthed the rest of the population, particularly her dear daughter's repugnant wastrel husband, who she was quite pleased to note was missing . . . 'With a bit of luck run over somewhere,' she thought with no smile.

A young and pleasant waitress appeared at the dining room door, 'If you would like, you can all be seated and we can serve you drinks at the table. Please come though when you are ready.' Slowly the family wandered in to the dining room and looked for their name cards, strategically planned so that Mrs Briarley's favourites sat opposite and next to her, with those she openly detested to the far edges of her vision. It wasn't long before Dave's absence was noticed due to the empty chair at the door end of the table. Mrs Briarley took this as an intended personal insult, my goodness she'd like to see him suffer, her hands twitched as if gripping him by his throat. 'Where is he then Beth, drunk, lost, asleep? Or have you come to your senses and left him at last. It's what I would have done a long time ago.' Some of the clan mumbled their conditioned approval, while others, fiddling with their napkins, kept an embarrassed silence, not wishing to be embroiled in the usual vitriol before having what they hoped would be a pleasant and digestible dinner.

Far away, along the beach and out of sight, Dave's mood swung wildly, from exhausted, resigned peace, tinged with hope of imminent rescue, (perhaps the phone had worked after all - it could be being traced and located as he lay there), to a sobbing helpless despair and desperation. The thought crossed his mind that a nearby broken bottle was almost within reach; one good effort and it would be in his hands, along with his own destiny. When the tide was closing in and no sign of rescue in sight he could cut off his foot at the ankle – or failing that – finish his life quickly with the broken glass to his throat.

Just as Dave was choosing his own dreadful destiny on the remote and deserted beach, so the Briarley family were choosing their favourite starters in the warm Georgian dining room of Hotel Astraea.

Dave's voice was beginning to fail and the adrenalin wear off, he shivered without noticing and his mind wandered into a day dream, to a place where he felt no pain. He was startled awake by a voice from somewhere behind him, a man's voice, calm, strong and confident, 'Hello, old chap, you seem to be in a bit of bother. Perhaps I can help.' And, as he moved closer into Dave's sight, 'My name's Harry, I'm from around here, spend a great deal of time at this old Royal Engineers pier myself you know, fascinating place.'

Dave thought of the worn path by the hole in the fence and put two and two together. 'Strewth, you made me jump Harry, so good to see another soul down here, I feared I was alone. I slipped and my ankle's stuck in the lattice work, it'll need cutting free I think.'

Harry carefully inspected the trapped ankle with an almost clinical interest, as though he was no stranger to such things, and then sat down close by Dave on a fallen steel girder. He spoke comfortingly with calmness and authority, 'you're not wrong there Dave, the authorities will have to bring some equipment to cut the steel. Meanwhile, try and relax the best you can, there's nothing more you can do about it. I'll stay with you all the way, so don't you worry about a thing.' Looking straight into Dave's half closed eyes, Harry lent forward, elbows on knees and concluded, 'You won't be the first that's done this. . . and I somehow doubt you'll be the last.' He smiled a little and gave a short reassuring laugh but none the less, Dave sensed an overwhelming empathy coming from Harry. Dave felt a warm sense of comfort flow over him, washing away all his fears, thank God he was saved. Harry's kind and somehow authoritative voice put him at ease, at peace. Dave looked at his rescuer with more than a hint of hero worship. Harry was a little shorter and younger than Dave but was powerfully built. Dave wouldn't be surprised if Harry was in the military in some capacity. Certainly, despite the horror of the situation Harry was taking it all in his stride, like he'd been there, seen that and done that all before. Dave felt blessed indeed that Harry had turned up, it was obvious now that the situation would be resolved satisfactorily and naturally.

Back at the Hotel there were blessings too. . . mostly for the size of the main course portions. The waitress noted that Dave's chair was still empty, 'Are we still waiting for someone? Shall I keep some of the servings back in case they turn up late?' She asked with a smile.

Beth started to speak but was beaten to it by her mother, 'No, you can clear away the place setting, he won't be joining us. We're here to have a good time, not worry about some waster with no manners.' One of his nieces, a kindly girl of good disposition towards him tried Dave's mobile number, perhaps she could send a covert warning of what was happening at the hotel, but only the messaging service kicked in, Dave was not answering wherever he was. They returned to the jolly matter of fine food and plenty of it, 'Good job Dave paid his share up front Beth dear,' confided her mother with a knowing, some might say patronizing look, 'You've wasted half your life on him, whatever was wrong with that nice boy you went out with before, whatever his name was?'

'I told him to be back mother, he's so uncaring and selfish, I hope it doesn't spoil your party,' Beth replied, already making private, vengeful plans for Dave's unhappy future. She would see he suffered as long as he lived for this embarrassment.

Harry looked across at Dave and smiled kindly, 'Don't worry Dave, all will be well in the end, you'll see, just have courage. Far beyond his ability to understand why,

Dave watched calmly as short, soft waves began to wash over Harry's feet. Dave was given comfort and strength by Harry's stoic resolution in the face of danger, that and the fact Dave had already exhausted himself with his earlier exertions. The onset of hypothermia was dulling some of his senses and the sea water that began gently lapping over his own feet seemed warm and agreeable, even welcoming.

At the hotel, puddings were being served to already stuffed stomachs, most of which were looking forward to a lie down on their beds for the afternoon. Beth was amazed at how much her mother could pack away, 'She was certainly a special woman, one to be admired,' Beth thought quietly.

'Hey! There's still money in the kitty . . . special coffees all round eh waitress,' shouted Nathan as small bits of fudge cake spattered the tablecloth in front of him - A grand end to a party.

At the beach, Dave thought of the party that he'd missed. He'd always been grateful for a good dinner and he was sorry he'd failed his wife and children by not being there for them. He imagined what Beth's mother would be saying about him . . . then he dismissed such negative thoughts. They just didn't seem appropriate for the moment and they certainly wouldn't help the situation. Warming soft waves gently lifted then covered more of his body now. Harry still sat on the nearby girder, water up to his waist but remaining resolute, still strong and with a compassionate yet empowering smile.

Dave was to feel no more pain from his trapped ankle and with his earlier plan for the broken glass long forgotten, he fell peacefully into his final sleep under the gentle rising water.

Postscript.

After being alerted by the landlady of Hotel Astraea, the authorities found and recovered Dave's body. It was the second time they had been to the old MoD site that year. Harry was quite right in what he'd said and they had to use cutting equipment to free Dave's leg too.

Beth left the car and all Dave's belongings at the hotel and travelled home with one of her children and her mother. They excitedly discussed divorce plans all the way. It was only when, a week later, a police officer called that Beth found out Dave's lifeless body had been found on the beach. 'Don't distress yourself too much, he wouldn't have known anything about it,' they said, 'it would have been over very quickly, he wouldn't have suffered,' they said.

Beth's mother smiled, now at last she could move in with her daughter and be looked after properly.

Dave sat with Harry beyond the fence on forbidden ground, they sat together on the girder chatting happily about old times when life was good and they watched with curiosity as twice each day the sea would cover them like a blanket, like the Gods covering a sleeping child from the cold.

At last, Harry was no longer alone. Perhaps one day someone else will join their party because they will always be there, waiting.

**

*'He who dies while he lives
shall not die when he dies.'*

**

Yenworthy and Countisbury

The welcomed stranger.

The tale of a young man's strange and supernatural adventure on Countisbury, where moor meets sea.

Sam was a tall, strong young man in his early twenties; staunch defender of a fiercely independent and self reliant nature, a trait he'd no doubt inherited from his Celtic ancestors.

Despite all his youth, strength and adventuring experience, as he approached from the Churchyard track, he was very happy to see signs of life and the early morning smoke rising from the chimney of the Blue Ball Inn, very happy indeed.

Though he was all night tired and hungry, he had a compelling tale to tell and tell it he must.

The landlord, an affable gentleman with a welcoming smile, observed him through the small casement windows as Sam crossed the road with determined gait and lengthening strides towards the Inn. The landlord slid the bolts and opened the heavy oak Inn door, a large long haired black dog stood curious at his side.

"I'm sorry sir, we don't open until later .....,"the landlord's voice trailed off as an inner voice told him something strange was afoot, his dog backed away silently and deeper into the old Inn, . . . "never you mind the time though sir, you come on in, come on in and sit yourself by the fire. . . we have some soup warming. . ."

Sam interrupted him, "Can it wait a while? I must tell someone what happened to me last night. . . someone must believe me. . . well to be honest I'm not certain what really happened at all, perhaps it was all a dream but then, how did I get here?"

"Here, sit you down there sir," reiterated the landlord, pointing to an upright wooden chair opposite an inglenook fireplace, the source of the smoke that had first welcomed Sam to Countisbury. The landlord carefully placed a fresh dry log and poked the fire thoughtfully; he asked, "So what's your name then sir, and what brings you to our door so early this winter's morning?"

"I'm Sam, Samuel Richmond, I should have been here last night. . . I've bed and breakfast booked here. . . " Sam forced a smile and a pretend laugh, "too late for the bed I suppose but I'd love a breakfast. . . but only when I've told you what happened first," said Sam.

The landlord nodded, held his hand up as if to say, 'one moment', then called towards the kitchen and his wife, "guest for breakfast dear, make it a big one." His wife poked her head through the open doorway by the bar, smiled, nodded in acknowledgement and disappeared again. "You'll not be disappointed Mr Richmond," the landlord assured, "so how is it you didn't arrive last night then?"

"Yesterday I was visiting friends over at Yenworthy Cottage, they're writers you know, well Robert is and his wife Beth is an archaeologist with a big university somewhere up north. They'd rented the cottage for six months, she's researching some old myths and legends about Viking raids along the Devonian coast and Robert is writing a book on the same sort of thing; he's calling it Dragon's Lair or was it Wolf's Lair. . . can't remember exactly, it's all made up stuff that he writes. . . but interesting none the less. I'd had a great day with them, a really interesting couple, passionate about their work. . . particularly Beth who couldn't wait to show me some old human bones she had recently unearthed, she obviously didn't consider it disturbing the peace of the dead. . .

it was just science to her. I stayed for a relaxed and pleasant lunch then we had a short walk to look at the sea. I was leaving it a bit late to get here by then and they told me I should stay overnight with them and walk here the next day in good light. But I didn't listen, I don't like to let people down and it's not more than a few miles along the coastal tracks. I collected my small overnight bag, nothing special in it and certainly nothing to equip me for the night that was to confront me and my sanity. Then I said my goodbyes to them, nearly for good too as it happened. I can't say I wasn't warned you know, they both said more than once I should be watchful for the sea mist coming in before dark and how dangerous it was along the combe edges. I told 'em straight, "don't you be worrying about me, I'll be fine, and such a stroll in the park won't be a problem for me." Well, I set off at a goodly pace along the wooded track towards the sea, all was going well, few ups and downs as you'll know but going Okay; the track was fairly clear to follow and I couldn't see it being a problem to arrive here either before or just after dusk.

I'd walked about an hour or more when it happened; in the blink of an eye the mist fell on me from all sides, as if it had been waiting in hiding for me, I couldn't see much at all, I lost sight of the track, in fact it was almost as though it vanished in front of my eyes, as if it wasn't there in the first place. I was committed by then, it was as bad or maybe worse to try and go back to Yenworthy. . . I have to confess I was filled with much regret and I'm not ashamed to say, a little fear, for the darkening night was cold and the mist was already eating into my bones. I knew well enough to keep away from the cliff edges and that I had perhaps three steep valleys to cross before I'd be out of the trees or come across the road. I was filled with such a sense of loss that it was as though nothing I knew existed anymore; my only proof of existence was a few feet of un-trod ground around me; No torch had I nor could I read my watch; I listened hard for the sound of the sea or of streams running seaward but the mist smothered all sound, I could hardly hear my own footfalls. I spoke loudly to myself, "Sam you idiot," I said, "you have done for yourself, now damn well get yourself out of this mess, come on get me out of here." God alone knows who I was talking to but talk I did. I knew I couldn't stay on the ridges but would have to drop down into a valley and up the other side. I thought that if trees could grow on the slopes then I could climb them too, it didn't work out like that, I made many small detours searching for invisible footholds with my blind feet while my cold hands grasped equally blindly for twigs or branches to keep my balance.

I was tiring quickly and the damp was truly biting bone deep, I began to feel the cold of the already dead. I'd always said I didn't need the help or advice of others, that I could do it all on my own but now a new truth was thrust upon me.

Half way up a steep and thicket strewn incline, my feet slipping on muddy slopes and thorns tearing at my clothes as if to hold me there, my legs began to fail and I thought to myself that this was the end of me; if they ever looked for or found my body they couldn't know the horrors that I felt last night. Then, as if by some magic, my feet found themselves on flat ground and I stood on a narrow ledge, my legs shaking a bit with exertion and adrenalin and me thinking I was losing my mind, hallucinating perhaps . . . but it was no illusion. . . there in front of me was a small stone and timber hut. . . and even better still, it was showing a light. With a fresh lease of life in body and in spirit I made my way to the hut and peered in through the wooden bars of a small glassless window; there was nobody in but a fire was burning in a simple earth hearth. I tried the door, it was primitive but opened well enough; I went in and sat on a bench like log near the fire and warmed my hands. . . oh, heaven it was to feel the mist dry out from my clothes and bones. I was sure that whoever lived there would return soon and I mentally prepared a little speech of thanks, apologies and the like that befits having entered someone's home uninvited. Though time seemed almost alien in that place, I glanced at my watch in the firelight; I cursed, it seemed to have stopped and it was a treasured gift from my long lost father. I put another log on the fire. . . there was a small stack near the bench within easy reach and a larger stack over by the far wall to my left. I sat in relative peace and calm with my speech in mind. . . the door opened and all my plans went out the window as I observed the owner of the hut standing in the doorway. He was shorter than us but stocky with one or two big scars on his bearded face, his hair nearly obscured his piercing eyes with a fringe that looked slightly reddish in the fire light, his clothes were simple and looked like he'd made them for himself from whatever he could find in the woods. He wore a stout leather belt which held an ancient looking axe at his side, his hand was on the axe shaft and his thumb caressed the curved blade. My speech had gone, not just what to say but the ability to say it too, I was gripped with fear. He came into the hut and closed the door, all the while looking in my direction and then he sat opposite me on a similar log bench like the one I was on. Still thumbing the axe blade he stared, almost as though he knew something that I did not, straight into my eyes. The only sound was my own breath and heartbeat. The fire began to die down and the room become darker, he gestured to me with his head and eyes to put another log on the fire, which I did so very carefully. God, I was tired, I have no idea what time it was or how long I'd been in the hut. I dared not sleep, I had to stay awake. The fire died down yet again and soon all the spare wood was used, I scraped together a few bits of bark and twigs and threw them on the fire which seemed as pleased as I to see the dancing flames warm the room. . . but soon they too were gone. As the hut cooled again, I went to stand and fetch a log from the other stack by the wall, as I did so, that stocky little man reacted sharply and gripped the axe handle as though to tell me to stay where I was . . . or else. . . or else I might die? Only God knows that answer.

Now and then the fatigue of exhaustion closed my unwilling eyes which would then be startled wide open by my fears, only to see the apparition still before me, his own ever wakeful and watchful eyes staring straight into mine. Try as I might I could not keep my eyes open and must have slipped into a deep and desperate sleep, and now, this is the strangest of all things, when I finally awoke to a chilly but mist free dawn, the strange man had gone, so had the fire, the logs and the hut, all gone.

I stood on the flat ledge and looked around in bewilderment. There, where the second log stack had been and which my intimidating and forbidding host had stopped me from reaching, there was nothing but space, a sheer drop to rocks and a stream far below. I would have fallen to my death; had I stepped there in the night for firewood, my broken body would have been meat for the rat, the fox and the raven.

Once the light of day had frightened the mist into the shadows I could so easily see my way forward and it wasn't so long before the path became clear all the way to the Inn. I left behind me on that flat ledge, thin grass mounds that still tell the world where walls once stood and perhaps, who knows, it was not so very long ago. I also left behind me eternal gratitude for a life saved, my own.

The landlord's wife called through that breakfast was ready and was to be had in the lower dining room. As Sam tucked into a hearty fried breakfast, the landlord suggested, "Your room is booked till midday, why not have a rest and stay for a pub lunch before moving on." The welcomed stranger was a welcomed guest once more. Sam nodded in agreement and glanced at his watch. . . he looked up and smiled. . . it was working again.

Author's note; I've revisited the Inn many a time and never heard the landlord speak again of that night, nor did Sam ever tell his tale to any other living soul. Sam left the Inn shortly after lunch and long before dark. He was not to be heard of again in these parts. Only you and whoever it is that inhabits the unearthly world of the sea mist know the truth. If I may be so bold, I suggest, if you know what's good for you, you will neither tell what you know, nor venture out when the sea mist threatens the night. Better you stay in and read a book by the inglenook. . . . you don't have to heed my advice.

**

"Experience is one thing you can't get for nothing" Oscar Wilde
**

And Finally...

From a conversation with a friend.

I was in the Inn early and before the Sunday dinners were ready. With a glass of wine in my hand, I chatted with the Innkeeper, a good man in all accounts. We talked of the strange entity that occasionally visited one particular table and how it made life so uncomfortably cold for one diner that he could not stay longer. Meanwhile the rest of the Inn had been pleasantly warm and welcoming.

Then he told me of a time when he lived in Canada. The houses there have large under floor spaces where they ran all the services, pipes, wires etc. Well, he had a leak somewhere and needed to go below floor to see what he could do to fix it. He gathered his tools and went to the trapdoor, then asked his young son of about four, if he wanted to join him. His young son was thrilled and as he had his own tools, you know the sort of thing, plastic hammer, plastic spanner, he proudly took them with him to work alongside his dad. The under floor area was not so well lit and the sloping ground a little rough but he located the leak and with a little concentrated effort was able to put it right. All finished and out through the trap door he closed it and went to pick up his tools. He then noticed that a particular wrench was missing, despite being very careful to pick everything up before returning above floor. He couldn't understand how he could have possibly missed it and turned to his son, asking, 'Did you see what happened to the wrench?'

The little boy answered. 'Yes dad . . the little old lady sitting in the corner took it.'

He never went back to retrieve his wrench. . . would you?

Printed in Poland
by Amazon Fulfillment
Poland Sp. z o.o., Wrocław